THE AUSTRIANS

The Austrians

STRANGE TALES
FROM THE VIENNA WOODS

Richard Bassett

faber and faber
LONDON · BOSTON

First published in 1988
by Faber and Faber Limited
3 Queen Square, London WC1N 3AU

Photoset by Parker Typesetting Service Leicester
Printed in Great Britain by
Richard Clay Ltd Bungay Suffolk

British Library Cataloguing in Publication Data

Bassett, Richard
The Austrians: strange tales from the Vienna Woods.
1. Austria—Social life and customs
I. Title
943.6'053   DB30
ISBN 0-571-13913-2
ISBN 0-571-15109-4 Pbk

For Boojum

Contents

Acknowledgements

This book could never have been written without the companionship of many Austrians who mercifully bear little relation to the characters encountered in the following pages. Herr Gottfried Pils, Gertrude Felderer and Rheinhold Geyer time and again prevented my view of Austria from becoming too jaundiced. I am particularly grateful to Countess Ines Thurn and Mrs Felicitas Trotsky (née Sachsen-Coburg-Gotha) for guiding me through the minefield which is the contemporary *Almanach de Gotha.* Countess Charlotte Szapary and her sister Tanya proved most supportive of my researches, while Katharina von und zu Liechtenstein reminded me that exceptions to the Austrian stereotype were not entirely unheard of, and that the tremendous excesses of the aristocracy were redeemed by the female of the species.

In England, Lucy Domvile and Celia de la Hey both struggled with my handwriting to ensure the manuscript reached the publishers on time. There Patrick Carnegy and John Denny offered sound advice and showed great patience.

Richard Bassett
Vienna, 1987

List of illustrations

Photographs reproduced by courtesy of *Profil* magazine, 1, 9, 12, 21,
26; Österreichische Nationalbibliothek, 2, 3, 7, 16, 17, 31; Archiv für
Kunst und Geschichte, Berlin, 4, 6; Österreichischefremdenvekehr-
werbung, 5, 14, 15, 18, 25, 27, 28, 29, 30, 32, 33, 34, 36; BBC Hulton
Picture Library, 8; Peter Philipe, 10; Votaphoto, 11; Österreicher
Verlag, 13; Kurt Molzer, 19; Heeresfilm- und Lichtbildstelle, 20; Adolf
Waschel, 22; Berthold Schmid, 23; Plankenauer, 24; and Otto Simoner,
35.

Foreword

In the course of some three and a half years as *The Times*'s correspondent in Vienna, I was often struck by the almost grotesque ignorance of the Anglo-Saxon of most things Austrian. Austria is one of the most visited countries in Europe, yet few people realize that the Austrians are very different from the Germans and the Swiss. Even fewer are familiar with the baroque combination of theatre and politics which passes for Austrian democracy. Myths and misconceptions about the glitter of Vienna and the precise role of the Austrians during the last war also abound.

In writing this book I have attempted to give a more realistic view, though not a definitive guide. It is of necessity something of a whirlwind tour, and I apologize in advance for any giddiness incurred.

At times the reader may find the sheer abundance of criticism levelled at the Austrians here somewhat daunting. No country is perfect, and the visitor to Austria is unlikely to encounter more than a fraction of the disagreeable experiences those *en poste* here are exposed to. These encounters are, as I hope to show, amply compensated for. None the less, in order to convey to the intelligent visitor something of the country's mentality, I have spared none of the darker side of the Austrian character. Only by an awareness of a nation's vices as well as its virtues can it properly be appreciated.

The reader may also be struck by the frequent recurrence of the theme of Austria's past. In no other country in Europe have the events of the eighteenth and nineteenth centuries left so powerful a legacy. The failure of the Austrians to shed old habits and attitudes is one consequence of the fact that Austria did not become a stable modern country until as recently as 1955. As a result I have felt obliged to burden the reader with extracts from works written earlier this century which perfectly describe characteristics that have survived unchanged despite the collapse of empire, two world wars and a ten-year occupation by the victorious powers. Of these authors Henry Wickham Steed, in whose shadow every Vienna correspondent of *The Times* scribbles, is the most important. His perception of the workings of the Austrian mind and of the capital city remains unrivalled.

Far from wishing to discourage people from visiting Austria, I hope that those who read this book will want to experience the considerable treasures, natural and cultural, in which it abounds. How better, though, to appreciate them than with an awareness of the mentality which in part fashioned many of those treasures.

But, like admiring some stupendous creation of the great Austrian architect Fischer von Erlach, a close look at the Austrians may send the senses spinning.

Richard Bassett
Vienna, 1986

CHAPTER I

What is an Austrian?

*'Austrians! An unsuccessful attempt to make
Germans out of Italians.'*
German officer during the Second World War

The German officer's quip epitomizes in its few exasperated
words the many misconceptions and prejudices that have
been laid at the door of the Austrians for centuries. The
implication that they are second-class Germans is clear.

Discussion of national characteristics is often littered with
such generalizations, and usually they contain an element of
truth. People who have never visited Austria tend to believe
that it is a rather less rigid and more charming nation than its
northern neighbour; that its centuries-old tradition of music
and the fine arts make it one of the bastions of European
culture; that its armies, unlike the disciplined and haughty
Prussians, rarely won any wars; and that its capital is witty,
urbane and gay whereas Berlin is cold, ruthless and militaris-
tic. In Paris after the war, to speak German was to invite
abuse from passers-by, but the words *'Mais je suis autrichien'*
sufficed to banish all hostility.

These flattering notions can be found in almost any
book written this century about the Austrians. Sometimes
praise of their virtues is diluted with apologetic reference to
the vices which are the inevitable reverse side of the coin:
with charm comes of course 'a weak character'; with spontaneity, 'unreliability'; with flexibility, 'incompetence'. *Homo
austriacus* is a complicated creature, whose temperament is
liable to infuriate the northern man just as easily as it can
seduce the northern woman, and some foreigners no doubt
wish that history had been more successful in fashioning

1

Germans out of the Austrians. To understand why they are not Germans, however, we must embark on a brief *tour d'horizon* of central Europe's history and geography and the Austrians' spectacular role at the forefront of that turbulent stage.

A look at the map of Europe shows at once that Austria lies on the crossroads of the continent, at the junction where Teuton meets Latin, Slav and Magyar. In the south-west the great Brenner pass through the fabulous peaks of the eastern Alps links Bavaria and Tyrol with the Italian plains. To the south-east is the ancient road to the Adriatic and Dalmatia. To the north-east that great artery of Europe, the Danube, winds its way down past Vienna towards the Balkans and the Black Sea through the great flat plain or *puszta* which resembles the awesomely forbidding eastern steppes. Different landscapes, different climates and, of course, different races, of which Austria became a veritable melting-pot. In no other part of the continent have the ethnic barriers been torn down and then reassembled with such frequency and violence.

The fact that the Austrians, like the inhabitants of Liechtenstein, speak German is perhaps the chief reason why the country has invariably been seen as part of the Teuton world. But, as the differences in temperament and mentality indicate, language is one thing, race quite another. German, the language of administration and the army in the early centuries of the Habsburg empire, welded tall Slavs, thick-set Alpine Celts and Nordic Germans into a cohesive and remarkably unified whole, absorbing as the years passed, Jews, Italians, Poles and even Russians. (One of the most prestigious Austrian fortresses was at Lemberg, now Lvov, in Russia.)

By 1918 and the collapse of the empire, few among the 6.75 million souls who were left stranded in the rump of the great Danube monarchy did not have at least one grandparent who was ethnically of different origins from the rest of their family. 'My grandma's Czech but my father was born in Budapest' is a familiar story. In Vienna today the telephone directory contains as many Czech names as that of Prague. In Prague, needless to say, there are almost as many German names as in Vienna.

Such a mixed people could never naturally have been moulded into 'Austrians', as opposed to Celts or Slavs, and to understand how they gave rise to one of the most powerful nations in history we must look at the Habsburgs.

Although it was Charlemagne in the eighth century who established the *Ostmark* – the Eastern Marches on the banks of the Danube – by destroying the Avar tribes, and though the Babenburg dukes enlarged the territory during their 270-year rule, it was Rudolf I (1218–91), the first of the Habsburg Holy Roman Emperors, who saw the enormous potential for consolidating and expanding its sphere of influence. In 1278 he defeated the Bohemian Premysl Ottokar near Vienna, and then set about subduing other neighbouring dukes and princes. Later Habsburgs, driven from their family strongholds in Switzerland by the exploits of men like William Tell, through a series of prescient dynastic marriages collected dukedoms and estates elsewhere with enthusiasm. In 1496 a Habsburg even married the heir to the Spanish throne. So successful was this Habsburg policy that it inspired the Latin tag '*Felix Austria, tu nube alii gerunt*' ('Happy Austria, you marry while others wage war'), a sentiment expressing perfectly a characteristic associated with the Austrians ever since – calculating but *au fond* unbelligerent. Nevertheless, while loth to resort to arms to expand their empire, the Habsburgs rarely failed to employ force to consolidate it.

The Reformation, with its cataclysmic upheavals, posed a threat to their Bohemian possessions which struck at the very heart of the empire. Czech-speaking Hussites expelled the Jesuits. In Prague two imperial envoys were dramatically defenestrated by Protestant nobles from the windows of Hradčany castle, and although they fell unharmed into a dung heap – a delivery attributed later by Catholics to a

3

miracle – this act of treason precipitated the Thirty Years War (1618–48). In 1620, at the Battle of the White Mountain, the flower of the Bohemian nobility was so utterly annihilated that it was not able to emerge again until almost three centuries later.

Almost a hundred years before that, in 1526, the Turks had dealt similarly with the Magyars at the Battle of Mohács, provoking the Habsburgs' attempt to fill the vacuum and confront the Infidel, and so beginning Austria's expansion down the Danube towards Budapest. With the destruction of the Bohemian nobility, the empire was consolidated to the north, but in the east a threat was still posed by the Turks. In 1683 an attempt by a large Turkish army to storm Vienna failed, thanks to the timely intervention of the dashing Polish Commander Jan Sobieski. The crescent standard never penetrated as far west again, and the Habsburgs began the long task of rolling the Turks back to Belgrade and beyond. By 1699 all of Hungary and much of Transylvania had been wrested from them, thanks to the brilliance of the Habsburg *Feldzugmeister* Prince Eugène of Savoy (1663–1736), whose exploits form one of the rare successful chapters in Austria's military history.

At the same time that this humbling of the Infidel defined Austria's role as a bulwark against the East, and the Counter-Reformation defended Catholicism in Europe, two important influences began to exert themselves on the Austrian character, influences which even today, long after the empire has disappeared, are still strongly felt.

The first of these was the Baroque, emanating from Italy and inspiring the great churches and palaces of Fischer von Erlach (1656–1723) and Lukas von Hildebrandt (1668–1745), which transformed battered Vienna into a fantastic stage on which the Holy Roman Emperor could walk against a backdrop of vast, awe-inspiring sets. Language as well as architecture became inflated, and the arts of improvisation and theatrical gesture became features of everyday life. At court these excesses flourished under a second exotic influence, the introduction of strict Spanish etiquette by Karl VI (1685–1740). This resulted in an obsession with regulations, titles and ancestry which continued long after the Habsburgs lost Spain and which still exerts a powerful hold over the Austrian mentality. Virtually every Austrian has a title: academics, journalists, accountants and even postmen and street cleaners, who are addressed as '*Herr Oberpostmeister*' or '*Herr Unterbezirkstrassenreinigungsrat*', or whatever title is appropriate. And most aristocratic families are still afflicted by a morbid fascination for family escutcheons and 'quarterings' – heraldic devices indicating family alliances – another legacy of the stifling influence Spanish etiquette had at court, where no one who was unable to boast sixteen quarterings was admitted.

Central to Austria's imperial status was the Catholic Church, whose influence, consolidated after the Thirty Years War, became a powerful ally of the monarchy. The emperor was the 'All Highest and Apostolic Majesty', and the divine rights of kingship became the theme of countless sermons in the vast Baroque churches which began to rise above the Vienna skyline.

Out of this world inhabited by rabid Jesuits, Baroque putti and bewigged courtiers appeared one of the most remarkable women in history, the Empress Maria Theresa (1717–80). Called to the throne in 1740 at the age of twenty-three, she found her empire menaced by a Prussia eager for the wealth of her province of Silesia; her army was virtually non-existent, her treasury bankrupt and her advisers, almost without exception, senile. But, perhaps more than any other Habsburg, she knew the Baroque art of improvisation. She tackled the situation with extraordinary energy, summoning new advisers and rallying the support of the Hungarian nobility. Legend relates how she won them over by dramatically holding up her infant son at her coronation in the Hungarian city of Pressburg (Bratislava) – an act well calculated to appeal to the Magyars' sense of chivalry and ensuring her the undying devotion of that rather temperamental race, though it did not save her from losing her beloved Silesia. By the end of her reign the empire was secure, her arch-enemy Prussia ruined if not beaten, and Austrian prestige higher than ever.

This combination of strength of character and intelligence occurs rarely among the Habsburgs, and it is no coincidence that it should have found expression in an empress rather than an emperor. In Austria it is often, though not always, the woman rather than the man who is the more inspiring.

If Maria Theresa proved what resources were available to the Austrian woman, her intelligent son and successor, Joseph II (1741–90), put into effect a number of reforms which, though overturned by his successors, were responsible for another inescapable feature of modern Austria – its bureaucracy. In fairness to Joseph, who was a more far-sighted monarch than any of his successors, this development was to a certain extent initiated by his mother, who sought to centralize the empire's power by concentrating it in Vienna. It fell to Joseph to develop this idea and ensure that an efficient administration, with its headquarters in the Austrian capital, was organized to administer the far-flung territories of the empire. These reforms laid the foundations for the vast civil service which ran the empire in the nineteenth century. Given that today's Republic of Austria has more civil servants per capita than the empire ever did, it can be seen that Joseph, although he ruled for only ten years, has much to answer for.

Leopold II (1747–92), who succeeded him, was a weak man though much loved in Tuscany, of which he was Grand Duke, but he ruled Austria for only two years. His successor was the conservative and authoritarian Franz II (1768–1835) who, after Napoleon's war against Austria resulted in the dissolution of the Holy Roman Empire, became Franz I. Four times he set himself against Napoleon's armies and four times he was soundly routed. But, keeping his head, he played for time, married his daughter Marie-Louise off to Napoleon and, in the end, had the satisfaction of seeing the Corsican ogre all but annihilated in 1813 at the Battle of Leipzig. At the Congress of Vienna his chancellor, Prince Clemens von Metternich (1773–1859), rapidly set about restoring the boundaries of pre-revolutionary Europe. Censorship and a secret police, in its methods and organization a milder forerunner of Hitler's Gestapo, ensured that any embers of liberal revolt were firmly extinguished.

Despite the despotism, the Congress promised stability and enabled frivolity to flourish. Franz, for all his authoritarianism, was not a hated monarch. At Baden, near Vienna, he built himself a large town house where he would walk freely among his subjects, the first of the Habsburgs to do such a thing. This was, after all, the so-called Biedermeier age, an age of domestic piety and bourgeois cosiness characterized by a *Gemütlichkeit* and charm which is still part of the Austrian temperament today. Characterized by comfortable villas, solid furniture and Schubert songs, few periods in history exuded such wellbeing and benign intention. Franz was a man of his time, with his fair share of charm, though in him, as often in intelligent people, it masked darker forces. Not far from his house in Baden is a fake medieval *Schloss* at Laxenburg, which Franz built to relive a less cosy age. In its dungeons there is a grotesque dummy prisoner who, if a particular stone is stamped on, will rattle his chains. Franz, who suffered many setbacks during his reign, can perhaps be excused for resorting to this rather macabre form of diversion.

In 1848, a year of revolution throughout Europe, the inevitable uprising against the repressive regime took place. Metternich was forced to flee (in a laundry basket, it is said) to England, and Franz's successor, the half-witted but amiable Ferdinand I (1793–1875), abdicated. He was succeeded by his good-looking nephew Franz Joseph (1830–1916) who, barely eighteen, settled down to rule for no less than sixty-eight years. A talent for improvisation, inherited from the Baroque era, was of enormous value during the upheavals of this reign, and *'fortwursteln'* – muddling through – was the byword of these years. Power was restored in the empire with the help of the army, though influence over Germany fell to Prussia after a disastrous six-week war in 1866. The Italian provinces were lost, save for Trieste; but in 1878 the chaos of Balkan politics, accompanying the decline of the Turkish empire, brought the Austrians compensation and a fateful advance in Bosnia and Herzegovina.

This Balkan thrust was quite logical. For decades what is now northern Yugoslavia had been ruled by the Habsburgs. Metternich himself had observed that Asia 'began on the Landstrasse', the once picturesque road running east from the centre of Vienna. Just as the Danube in medieval times was responsible for the spread of the Gothic style from central Europe to southern Yugoslavia, so the road to the Balkans was the means by which many 'oriental' practices were able to penetrate the heart of Catholic Europe and flourish in Vienna. Bribery, nepotism, corruption, the unpredictable and sudden enforcement of statutes normally ignored – these essentially Balkan traits have all lingered in Austria, and are partly responsible for that slap-dash, happy-go-lucky quality which so infuriates the Germans.

At the same time that the empire was expanding in the Balkans, there arose in Vienna another trait, resulting from expansion in a different area, which has lingered with the Austrians. Since the eighteenth century, when the Habsburgs acquired Galicia (now part of Russia and eastern Poland), Jews had poured into Vienna in search of improvement and fortune. By the mid-nineteenth century they were well represented in the financial, literary and artistic worlds. This provoked hostility in many circles, which found expression in the late nineteenth century in the writings of Georg von Schönerer (1842–1921) and Karl Lueger (1844–1910), the firebrand mayor of Vienna. Hitler made use of both these men's writings, and it is often overlooked that Austria's anti-Semitism predates that of the Third Reich. But this is to anticipate. Other dramatic events were now at hand. As is so often the case in Austria's history, it was events elsewhere that initiated change.

In 1914, on St Vitus's Day, the heir to the throne, Archduke Franz Ferdinand and his wife were shot by a young Bosnian anarchist with links with a Serbian movement known as the Black Hand. A few weeks later, in Bad Ischl, the aged Emperor Franz Joseph 'for reasons of honour' signed the Declaration of War which was to see the end of three empires. Four years later, when the Imperial Army was finally ripped apart by war on three fronts, modern Austria was born geographically if not politically.

The chaos which followed the unhappy treaties of St Germain and Trianon, which left thousands of Germans in Italy and millions of Hungarians in Romania, is well known. It led inevitably to the revival of German militarism and, more importantly, it provoked an intense contempt for England, once Austria's most steadfast ally. The First World War was the first and last occasion the two empires entered into hostilities with each other, though Austrian and British troops did not come face to face during the fighting.

Before the war the climate of opinion in Britain and America, and the belief that the Austrian empire must be dismantled, was largely created by the writings of two Englishmen: Henry Wickham Steed, Vienna correspondent and later editor of the London *Times*, still a name familiar to many Austrians, was one of these Cassandras; Professor R. W. Seton Watson was the other. Both believed that the empire had no future and that the twenty peoples the Habsburgs ruled would have to gain their independence one day, but both failed to realize that the vacuum in central Europe caused by dismantling the Habsburgs' power would be filled by more oppressive forces. It would be difficult to overestimate the effect these two gifted men had on turning intelligent opinion in Austria against Britain after the First World War.*

*How well I remember being passionately upbraided at a ball by a sixteen-year-old pupil because I worked for the newspaper that 'spawned Wickham Steed'.

Deprived of her main agricultural supplies from Hungary, her principal industries in Bohemia and her port at Trieste, Austria survived the war remarkably well. A post-war Socialist government banned the Habsburgs and the use of aristocratic titles and initiated a series of apartment-building projects which soon became the envy of Europe. Their Marxist ideals, however, unnerved the nobility and the Catholic peasantry who, with Fascist support, took up arms against the Socialists. In 1934, in a brief but bloody conflict, the army and Fascist elements bombarded and demolished many of the recently constructed apartment blocks. From this arose a fierce class hatred which is noticeable in one form or another even in today's 'egalitarian' Austria, where terms like 'proletariat' enjoy a greater currency than in supposedly more class-conscious countries like France and Britain.

A clerico-Fascist regime was established under the Federal Chancellor Engelbert Dollfuss (1892–1934), and the democratic experiment begun so optimistically after the First World War was extinguished. It is important to realize that few Austrians cared about this. Under the Habsburgs, Parliament had become a circus where the blowing of horns and brawling were more frequent than serious debate. For the Austrian on the Prater tram it was far more important that the administration functioned.

It was partly because of this that many otherwise intelligent Austrians saw Hitler as a saviour. He would restore the pensions their grandmothers had lost with the collapse of the empire. He would ensure work for the unemployed. There would be *Ordnung*.

Though resisted by some Austrians, the *Anschluss* – the annexation by Germany of Austria – and Hitler's triumphant entry into Vienna and Graz were on the whole well received, and Austrians served gallantly alongside Germans during the next four years of carnage. Some – a surprisingly high proportion – proved shamefully over-zealous in their duties while serving with the SS. It is sad to relate that proportionately more Austrians manned concentration camps than Germans.

Between the end of the war and 1955, Austria was administered by the four victorious allied powers. This had a number of far-reaching effects. One was a general stultifying of initiative. Another was a deep-rooted distrust of Communism. A third was the encouragement of Austrian patriotism. Austrians remain justly proud that of all the countries occupied by the Russians after the war, theirs is the only one to have seen the back of them. The negotiations which led to the Russians leaving Austria in 1955 were tortuous, and luck played its role. Had the Hungarian Uprising of 1956 occurred a year earlier, it is unlikely that the Russians would have agreed to leave. That they did allowed a small country to acquire a freedom and democracy which had long eluded it.

Prosperity swiftly followed, and with it the perhaps inevitable forsaking of spiritual for material values. Now, after thirty years of social and political stability, a national identity has emerged which makes people proud to be Austrians and not Germans; proud of their charm and even of their flexibility or incompetence. Proud, too, of their imperial patrimony, for there is considerable nostalgia for the grandeur if not the precepts of the empire. Perhaps it is because democratic Austria is so recent, and the Habsburg past so long and glorious, that this backward-looking mentality exerts such a powerful influence.

CHAPTER II

An Eastern contribution
to Western culture

*'When we think about life seriously, we have to
admit home is for all of us the
Vienna Musikverein.'*

Die Presse, 1985

The historical and geographical factors which created a
nation quite distinct from the Germans played a no less
important role in fashioning a mentality peculiarly well dis-
posed towards the arts. Proximity to the Orient, the extravagant racial mix and, perhaps above all, the existence in Vienna
of a single, prosperous urban centre on the crossroads of
Europe, all helped to produce conditions in which the arts
could flourish.

No part of Europe was as productive in the sphere of music
as Vienna was between 1781, when Mozart (1756–91) settled
in the Habsburg capital, and 1828, when the death of
Schubert (b. 1797), following closely on that of Beethoven
(1770–1827), brought the city's classical era to an end. This
musical Parnassus was in part the result of Vienna's position
as the capital of an empire unrivalled in the western world.
As the great palaces which line the city's Herrengasse testify,
more than in any other city in central Europe, the Viennese
aristocracy vied with each other in securing the services of the
best architects, painters and musicians.

Some, like Haydn (1732–1809), who was *Kapellmeister* to
the Esterházy family at nearby Eisenstadt, had to persuade
their masters – by gaining international recognition more
than anything else – that they should be treated as more than
mere footmen. Others, like Mozart and Beethoven, had to
eke out a meagre living as performers. But it was in Vienna

that they became 'great composers', as did Mahler (1860–1911) and Bruckner (1824–96) later in the century. Ironically, though, while it might be fair to say that Bruckner would never have become as inspired had he remained in Linz, nor Mozart so brilliant had he continued to live in Salzburg, the Viennese themselves, with few exceptions, did not recognize until much later what genius had resided in their midst.

If, as has often been contended, great art needs the stimulation of a crass and philistine public to scale the heights of immortality, then Vienna, throughout the late eighteenth and nineteenth centuries, provided this in abundance. Although Haydn was revered in old age – when Napoleon entered Vienna in 1809 he immediately placed as a token of respect a sentry on the house of the dying composer – both Mozart and Schubert died impoverished and virtually unnoticed by the Viennese.

By the 1850s, however, the Viennese had come to recognize something of their unique musical heritage, and musicians flocked to the city for employment and inspiration. Conductors from Slovenia, pianists from Moravia, all believed – quite correctly, from the material point of view at least – that success meant making one's name in Vienna. And so the tradition continued until the Second World War, when the division of Europe deprived Vienna of its eastern lifeblood and eyes turned to London, which had accepted so many refugees, often Jewish, to assume responsibility as the repository of Europe's culture.

In Vienna today this great musical tradition is preserved by two unique institutions, both of which are remarkable in a country of less than eight million people. The first is the Vienna Staatsoper which, despite a well-deserved reputation in recent years for static and dull productions, continues to offer audiences on a good night the combination of excellent singers and the most distinguished orchestra to be found in any opera pit in the world – the Vienna Philharmonic. The second is the Musikverein, a handsome neo-classical concert house with an unsurpassed acoustic,* where on Sunday mornings the Vienna Philharmonic performs its inimitable interpretations of the great classics. A considerable aura surrounds this building, and subscription tickets, handed down from generation to generation, are a source of great pride among conservative Austrians.

No one who has heard Beethoven, Brahms or Bruckner played by the orchestra which was nurtured by Hans Richter, Weingartner and Furtwängler could possibly imagine another orchestra sounding more suitable. However, it is not a sound which copes well with the modern classics like Stravinsky or Benjamin Britten. Like Austrian music itself, which can be said to have passed away as a world force with the death of Berg (1885–1935) and the emigration in 1933 to America of Schoenberg (1874–1951), the Vienna Philharmonic is not at ease with the post-war world. Not surprisingly, its weakest section is perhaps its heavy brass, which is rarely required to rise to the virtuoso challenge of a Walton symphony or a Stravinsky ballet. But these are minor criticisms of one Austrian institution which can hold its own in the world.

If Austria has spawned a unique musical heritage, its performance in the other arts has been no less impressive, although the ease with which music can cross political frontiers and language barriers will perhaps ensure that it is for music rather than theatre that Austria remains most renowned. Partly because of this, it is often thought that the Austrian is a born musician. This is an extravagant misconception, as anyone who has spent five minutes at a service in an Austrian village church will testify. Unlike England, where centuries of choral tradition continue to allow Sundays to resound with Anglican sung evensong, Austria, despite the ubiquitous Vienna Boys' Choir, is not a country where choral singing flourishes. In few cities is amateur music so disappointing as

*An acoustic curiously unfavourable to orchestras whose strings are not top notch, as many London orchestras have found.

in Vienna. Acting, on the other hand, can be seen at every street corner and café. Caricature becomes reality when a waiter argues with his customer about the amount of milk in his coffee. Since the demise after the last war of much that was great in Austrian theatre, the traditon can be seen to flourish in dramas enacted on the Ringstrasse:*

'Drunkard! Oaf! Idiot! Can't you see where I'm parking!'

'Go to the devil! Drunkard! Just because I can see you, you don't have to do it, do you!' etc . . .

In this respect Vienna is unrivalled. Posturing, exaggeration, threats which instantly crumple up into spineless submission when encountering the slightest resistance – these are the stuff of Johann Nestroy (1801–62), the great Austrian Biedermeier playwright whose taste for irony expressed so much of the Viennese mentality. The Austrians are born improvisers, happy to storm with rage one moment but equally content to smile innocently the next. Nestroy's relentless exposure of human weakness through a macabre humour, which at times is almost sinister, reflects characteristics familiar to anyone who has lived in Vienna or Graz or even as far west as Salzburg for any length of time, though the wit of Nestroy's world has been replaced by a sullen misanthropy in many places. Later in the century, this exposure of emotions was further highlighted in the dramas of Arthur Schnitzler (1862–1931), who added to it his characters' own peculiar strain of coquetry and promiscuity.

A mercurial but *au fond* weak temperament and a short-fuse temper are often accompanied by promiscuity. To a certain extent climate and geography are to blame. A dry and scorching summer and a long freezing winter encourage a certain amount of self-indulgence and a tendency to remain indoors. The proximity of eastern Europe and the presence of a vast former peasantry which, though emancipated,

---

*This native talent for drama flourished in Hollywood which after the First World War was virtually constructed by Austrian émigrés, of whom Fritz Lang and Erich von Stroheim were only two.

retains certain peasant values – shoes are almost always removed when entering an Austrian home – encourages this. In northern Europe such values virtually died out in the nineteenth century, but here, nourished by both materialism and Socialism, they have proved remarkably resilient. Schnitzler's plays often feature as a heroine a young girl of working-class origins and essentially peasant values. Sweet, charming, naïve, but also cunning and, invariably, highly sexed, such girls can be found anywhere in Austria today.

It should not be thought from this that Austrian drama and literature at the turn of the century were concerned entirely with sensual love. While Schnitzler was writing his tales of philandery, in a castle above what was then the Austrian Riviera, at Duino, near Trieste, a young romantic was proclaiming through his poetry a taste for the ideals of platonic affection, albeit littered with some perverse imagery. The elegies of Rainer Maria Rilke (1875–1926), written at the beginning of this century, breathe a mysticism far removed from the everyday absurdity inherent in Schnitzler's works. For Rilke 'every angel is terrible', and beauty reflects only horror. His poetry, so often branded as decadent, represents three characteristic Austrian qualities: an almost sensual passion for the possibilities of the German language; a predilection towards melancholy tinged with hopelessness; an almost oriental fatalism; and, above all, an enthusiastic delight in the grotesque and the art of paradox. The heroism in his writing is all the more telling for the fact that, as Stefan Zweig relates, the young Rilke was a most delicate fellow for whom the exploits of his dashing 'Cornet Christopher Rilke' would have been unthinkable. Zweig (1887–1968), whose memoir *The World of Yesterday* (1942) sums up so many of the contradictions of Vienna at the turn of the century, recalled how during the war the young Rilke found even the safe job of archivist almost too much of a strain on his highly strung sensibilities. Rupert Brooke at least died in the Mediterranean *en route* for Gallipoli. Rilke refused to contemplate any such chance of a distasteful end, and remained safe in his archives.

As well as Schnitzler and Rilke, a third distinguished figure occupied the stage of Austrian literature before the great crash in 1918. Karl Kraus (1874–1936), a journalist and satirist, was, like many artists of imperial Austria, a Jew (though baptized a Catholic). His writings, like Rilke's, display a passion for the German language, going so far as to ascribe high moral importance to the precision with which he felt it should be used. This combined with a penetrating analysis of what the Austrian mind was capable of in terms of crassness, prejudice and primitive hysteria. Curiously, as well as these acerbic traits, Kraus was also capable of that other quintessentially Austrian characteristic, nostalgia. When Claudio Magris, arguably the most perceptive present-day critic of Austrian culture, wrote a doctoral thesis for the university of his native Trieste based on the celebration of the Austrian empire in twentieth-century literature, he found to his surprise that whereas not a single novel or poem of value dating from before the 1914 war could be found glorifying the lumbering multi-racial Danube monarchy, as soon as it disappeared in 1918 a flood of books began to appear commemorating that lost world. Even Karl Kraus, so critical of the inefficiency, pretentiousness and cruelty of old Austria, described its end as 'the last days of mankind'.

Joseph Roth (1894–1939), another Jew, more gently if less convincingly evoked the old order with stories like the *Radetzky March* and *The Capuchin Vaults*, which exude a starry-eyed nostalgia comparable to an alcoholic haze in its distortion of realities. Another Austrian writer, Alexander Lernet-Holenia (1897–1976), stirred up the central European's capacity for nostalgia even further in a series of highly readable and popular but ultimately limited novels about the last days of imperial Austria's army.

Such a proliferation of backward-looking literature is unrivalled in the twentieth century – though there are some parallels in the recent nostalgia in Britain for the Raj – and it goes a long way to explain the present-day Austrian's preoccupation with the past. Of course it is not necessary for an

Austrian to read a book in order to become acquainted with his country's history: every street in the centre of any Austrian city points the eye to the past rather than the future.

Architecture, rather than literature, is the second great cultural achievement for which Austria is internationally renowned. There are no Gothic monuments that can stand comparison with those of Normandy or England, but during two periods in European history Austria produced architects who focused the architectural world's attention on the city of Vienna.

The first was the Baroque era, which imbued the Austrians with a taste for artistic hyperbole. The leaders of the Counter-Reformation, both clerical and aristocratic, proved generous patrons, and this period saw the establishment of a series of buildings which must rank among the finest in the world. In particular, two architects appeared who were able, in the course of about fifty years, to immortalize their names in the history of architecture.

Much time could be spent pondering the relative merits of Johann Bernhard Fischer von Erlach and Johann Lukas von Hildebrandt, the two giants of the Austrian Baroque. Both were masterly exponents of the art of playing inventively with space, and both explored the language of Roman Baroque to a degree which would have made any self-respecting Italian architect blanch. Hildebrandt's extraordinary summer palace, the Belvedere, built in Vienna for Prince Eugène of Savoy, added to the usual vocabulary of domes and caryatids the forms of the Turkish tents which had surrounded Vienna during the siege of 1683. Fischer, in the staircase of the winter palace in the Himmelpfortgasse for the same master, extended a few years earlier, produced motifs which in their grotesque intentiveness would have been seen by Borromini or Bernini as bordering on the insane.*

---

*This taste for the exotic and the grotesque remains in the Austrian character, and is evident in a debased form, on a different level, in many of the so-called quality stores to be found in Vienna today, where fashion shops for the last two years have insisted on promoting poison green and lurid orange as 'the beautiful colours' of the season.

Unlike Jakob Prandtauer (1660–1726), a native of Tyrol and Austria's third great Baroque craftsman, responsible for the imposing abbey at Melk, Fischer and Hildebrandt were architects rather than builders. Their theories were developed from the latest teaching in Rome and it was left to Fischer, with his treatise on historical architecture, *Entwurf einer historischen Architektur* (1721), the first serious history of architecture to be published in Europe, to lay the foundation of what was later to become the touchstone of Austrian architecture's traditional strengths – a school of rational theory. 'A maverick without immediate progeny', in his wide interest in the architects of other ages and continents Fischer represented a cosmopolitan departure from the introspective, provincial school of Austrian architecture. In the Karlskirche in Vienna he created a monument to this international thinking by mixing classical Roman with Turkish and even neoclassical ideas. Although easily surpassed in technique by the buildings of the great Roman architects, it has an imperial brilliance which none of them rivalled.

The influence of the Baroque in Austria was formidable. Every Gothic church was refitted with Baroque altars and chandeliers, madonnas and crucifixes. Not surprisingly, neoclassicism, that altogether cooler style, though present in a diluted Biedermeier form, barely got off the ground,* and the next great period of Austrian architecture that merits attention came in the late nineteenth century, when the bombastic palaces of the Ringstrasse had almost completed ringing the changes in every possible style. Exhausted by this eclecticism, a new school of architecture arose which was anti-establishment and prepared to shock as much as the Baroque had excited.

Jugendstil, Austria's *art nouveau*, was not, however, an entirely revolutionary style, and, though prolific, it produced few buildings of any real beauty. It grew in part out of the gentle classical forms of the Biedermeier period, while in its

*In striking contrast to neighbouring, more Protestant, Hungary.

fondness for opulent façades and the curved line it has a kinship with the Viennese Baroque. The same indulgence and delight in superficial effects can be seen in the *femme-fatale* façades of the 1890s in Graz and Vienna.

None the less, some architects, notably Adolf Loos (1870–1933), who despised *Jugendstil*, and Otto Wagner (1841–1918), who was perhaps more of an engineer than an architect, rose above the decorative but mediocre works produced at this time, and became, like Fischer von Erlach before them, forceful exponents of a style they believed must be international.

Loos looked in particular towards Anglo-Saxon culture for inspiration. The primitive, backward, narrow-minded and tasteless Austrian is constantly lambasted in his writings. His belief that elegance stems from function rather than from decoration extended even to clothing, and he admired the practical dress of the English gentleman in Hyde Park on a Sunday afternoon. His cogent arguments against the debasing of Anglo-Saxon taste in Austria are just as relevant today, and he would have been horrified to see the lurid tweeds and curiously-cut suits which fill Austrian shops boasting names such as 'Lord John', 'Sir Anthony' and 'The Home of the English Fleet'.

Otto Wagner was also inspired by certain English developments, though he never thought to extend architectural taste into every aspect of life in the way Loos did. Both architects, however, produced buildings which must be counted as pioneers of modern taste in architecture, yet while they are widely appreciated among modern architects, their names are not known by a broader public. This is a pity, as there can be no doubt that it is largely due to the legacy of Loos and Wagner that Austria's brilliance in the field of modern architecture has sustained itself in the 1980s.

Standing opposite the Hofburg on the Michaelerplatz in Vienna, gazing at Loos's green marbled columns and lidless windows, it is difficult to imagine that the structure dates from as early as 1906. It stirred sufficient horror among the

Viennese that the Archduke Franz Ferdinand, who walked occasionally opposite it in the Hofburg, is said to have commented that if he met Loos he would happily break every bone in his body. History does not record whether Loos felt some relief when, a few years later, the archduke fell victim to a Bosnian anarchist's bullet at Sarajevo.

Today, architects justly acknowledged outside Austria as being among the finest of their generation in the world are still snubbed by those controlling the purse-strings of public patronage. Herr Hans Hollein, perhaps the best known of Vienna's gifted new school of architects, had built museums in Germany long before he was offered anything more substantial than a candle shop in Vienna. Hollein, Holzbauer and Boris Podrecca, household names in the tightly knit fraternity of international architecture students, remain virtually unknown to the Viennese, some of whom in 1986 even protested around the building site of Hollein's first proper commission in Vienna (the site, opposite St Stephen's cathedral, still stands empty because of planning difficulties).

For a country that enjoys some of the finest vernacular buildings in the world, it is remarkable that it should go to such lengths to destroy many which do not attract tourists. No conservation lobby exists in Austria, and in the suburbs of Vienna countless Biedermeier buildings are being ripped to pieces at the behest of companies eager to erect colourless but profitable flats. In some cases a façade is preserved but the magnificent courtyards are frequently destroyed. The seventeenth-century Palais Wallner in the Wallnerstrasse, for instance, lost its eighteenth-century courtyard and acacia tree in a hideous redevelopment, and the even more precious houses of the Gardegasse have now been demolished. Despite the gifts of some modern Austrian architects, there are many who seem happy to acquiesce in this destruction.

In painting and sculpture the situation is even bleaker. Though Austria has some of the finest paintings in the world hanging in its galleries, few painters of international repute have been born in Austria. The Baroque era produced talented but mostly second-rate painters, whose principal task was often to 'adorn' the creations of the architects. During the Biedermeier period, Waldmüller (1793–1865), a watered-down Pre-Raphaelite with a taste for depicting children in *Lederhosen*, and Moritz Schwind (1804–71) are two painters whose works merit perhaps a second glance. Rudolf von Alt (1812–79), a fine watercolourist, is another artist of this period whose work is easy on the eye. But none of these would merit inclusion in a desert-island gallery.

A hint of what was to come in the so-called Viennese Secession period is given by the curious paintings of an artist called Anton Romako (1832–89). His painting, in Vienna's Belvedere gallery, of the Austrian flagship *Erzherzog Max* about to ram the Italian frigate *Re d'Italia* at the Battle of Lissa in 1866, is one of the most vivid and bizarre portrayals of a naval battle in existence.

The emotions Romako hints at are fully expressed in the works of Gustav Klimt (1862–1918) and Egon Schiele (1890–1918), two painters who alone are responsible for bringing Austrian art to the attention of art-lovers throughout the world. Klimt, in his famous golden portrayal of *The Kiss*, and Schiele, in his distorted pictures of naked bodies, did more than anyone involved in Austrian literature or music to create the image of Viennese *fin-de-siècle* decadence. Certainly both were capable of expressing in a drawing or a canvas the essential sensuality of Austrian women and the power struggle which so overtly marks many Austrian relationships, a factor which was more cerebrally explored by Freud, many of whose patients were the subjects of these *femme-fatale* portraits.

Though decadence is, even today, very much associated with Vienna, it should not be accepted unquestioningly. As Sir Ernst Gombrich, himself of Viennese origins, has observed, there is too much talk about decadence when the topic of Vienna is raised: 'Just because people sat around in coffee houses it does not mean that they were decadent.'

The brief but highly charged flowering of Austrian painting which took place with the development of Klimt and Schiele died as swiftly as it began, leaving only Oskar Kokoschka (1886–1980) to continue the Viennese tradition. Significantly, he chose to do so away from Austria, in London.* He was perhaps the last link with this rich tradition, for although some of his pupils have returned to Vienna, the stream has been interrupted.

This state of affairs is partly the result of events which took place in Austria between 1938 and 1945. Significantly, the Jewish population in Vienna, a sizeable community which played so great a part in Austria's cultural life before the war, was almost entirely lost after the Holocaust to London and New York. It is to their controversial role in Austria's history that we must now turn.

---

*The Austrians' ambivalent attitude towards their artists was recently illustrated when the celebrated London Kokoschka exhibition, which travelled to Prague and America, was spurned by the Viennese authorities.

CHAPTER III

Anti-Semitism and the Jews

*'In the company of young aristocrats I had sampled
the night life of Vienna. After the nth bottle I heard
them make a feeble attempt to raise the old pre-war
cry of "Raus mit den Juden" (Out with the Jews!).
It was a curious reminder of the fact that the ideo-
logy of anti-Semitism had its birth in Vienna.'*
R. Bruce Lockhart, *Retreat from Glory* (1939)

May 1986, the Leopoldstadt. A group of orthodox Jews
dressed in sombre black with corkscrew curls is about to cross
the road when a car screeches to a halt. The startled walkers
have panic written all over their faces. The driver apologizes.
He saw the red light too late. No one is hurt, but their look of
fear is not easily forgotten.

Before the war the Leopoldstadt, Vienna's Second District,
was the home of over 180,000 Jews. Today there are barely
8,000, and their synagogue here is one of the few to have
survived in Austria. In those balmy May days, amid an international furore surrounding the candidature in the presidential election of Dr Kurt Waldheim, because of his wartime
career as a lieutenant in the German *Wehrmacht*, they are
witnessing some of the most virulent anti-Semitism Austria
has experienced since the Third Reich.

Less than a year later, when the remarkable outcome of
that most bitterly contested of Austrian presidential elections
had been largely forgotten by the world, the US decision to
bar him from visiting America merely resurrected an issue
most Austrians believed buried. But the vehemence of the
emotions aroused has not been forgotten by the Jews who live
in Austria and who have had to face the unpalatable fact that

24

for the first time since Adolf Hitler anti-Semitism has been used for political ends. Although Dr Waldheim and those who support him have denied this, there can be no doubt that in the charged atmosphere of his election certain statements and slogans were uttered which could only be interpreted as anti-Semitic.

Many Austrians are, in fact, quite openly anti-Semitic. A small minority go so far as to send poison-pen letters to Jewish organizations in Vienna and daub such phrases as *'Juden raus'* ('Jews out') on walls, public lavatories and monuments. Most, however, are content with making snide comments, cracking jokes and treating the very idea of the Jews with undisguised contempt.

Anti-Jewish jokes are of course not the preserve of the Austrians. Nevertheless, Austrian anti-Semitism must be distinguished from that of other European countries for two reasons. First, the fact that it has survived despite the virtual extinction of the Jews as an influential force in Austrian art, the press and, most important of all, finance. Secondly, the fact that Austria generated some of the most persuasive anti-Semitic propaganda the world has ever seen, propaganda which fell on the eager ears of Adolf Hitler. Had he been a German instead of an Austrian, and grown up far from Vienna, the city he always regarded as *'verjudet'* ('Jewified'), there can be little doubt that the Nazis' orgy of Jew-hating which took place in the 1930s would have lacked much of its ideological and emotional force. It could even be speculated that it might never have taken place at all, for with the exception of Bavaria in southern Germany, the hatred for the Jews which is so much a part of the Austrian empire's history was much less evident in nineteenth-century Germany.

In order to understand why it is that anti-Semitism has survived in a country with one of the smallest populations of Jews in Europe, and why millions of people living at the fountain-head of European culture were prepared to stand by and see thousand of people they knew, and indeed were even friends with, abused, humiliated and murdered, it is once again necessary to examine the past.

The history of the Jews in Austria and central Europe is long and complex. In the seventeenth century, long before Hitler employed the yellow star to distinguish Jews from Germans, the Austrians had forced the Jews to wear yellow and live in ghettos where their homes were regularly searched by authorities who were empowered to do so by a special statute. Hatred and contempt for the Jews continued into the nineteenth century, when a philosophical and literary anti-Semitism developed in the writings of Georg Schönerer (1842–1921) and his contemporary Karl Lueger (1844–1910), who saw in the Jews a threat to Western culture.

In 1848 Jews had been allowed for the first time in the history of the Austrian empire to own land, and in 1867 they were granted further rights which allowed a flourishing Jewish middle class to emerge and play a significant part in the development of the empire from a backward, pre-industrial country into a more advanced society. (Up to that time Austria, still essentially feudal, did not have that important agent of economic progress, a bourgeoisie.)

Not that all Austria's Jews were well-to-do. Many were in the last stage of degradation and exploitation, and by 1914 300,000 had emigrated to America and England to escape poverty. But those who were prosperous and gifted enough to raise themselves above this state needless to say aroused the bitterest hatred. In the cities their propensity for making capital and their enthusiasm for speculative projects resulted in a number of unpleasant consequences for any businessmen who competed against them. Savage price-cutting and the use of sweated labour put whole streets of gentile artisans out of work. Their sporadic and sudden profits promoted instability on the stock market and a number of crashes occurred which left many gentile businessmen penniless.

In the country an indolent aristocracy was happy to place

the management of their estates in the hands of a Jewish manager, who would drive the labourers to the very extremes of physical endurance in order to allow the absentee landlord to gamble another few thousand crowns a night in the casinos of Vienna or Budapest. As a usurer this Jewish factotum made himself doubly unpopular by forcing slow-witted peasants into a situation whereby when a harvest failed they inevitably had no other recourse than to borrow money from their manager. Punitive rates of interest, as high as 500%, meant that the peasants were in debt for years afterwards.

From this it can be seen that anti-Semitism in Austria was essentially based on economic rather than racial resentment. This feeling was reinforced, if only slightly, by the predominance of Jews in the press. Austrian journalism before 1918 produced some of the best-written and most astringent articles published anywhere in Europe, but as Wickham Steed, editor of *The Times* in the 1920s, pointed out while correspondent for that paper in Vienna before the Great War, 'When, as in the Habsburg Monarchy, the press is entirely Jewish, the press deprives the Jews of the educational influence of fair criticism and removes from their path those minor checks and warnings that might otherwise induce them to practise the, for them, supremely difficult virtues of self-restraint and moderation' (*The Habsburg Monarchy*, 1914).

That these words were written not by an Austrian but by one of the most astute observers of Austrian life before the First World War, and one whose integrity and impartiality were above question, shows how easily anti-Semitism could penetrate the minds of the intelligent and those whose cool northern upbringing would, one might imagine, render them impervious to such prejudice. But it also shows the extent to which Jews dominated the Austrian press, and how this domination aroused the hostility of the most impassive and unhysterical observers. More Wickham Steed: 'Centuries of segregation and – as regards the mass – of pauperism, working upon non-European temperaments, have prevented the Jews from knowing instinctively how much Jewish influence a non-Jewish public will tolerate. They unconsciously violate the unexpressed canons of non-Jewish taste and are filled with amazement and a sense of injustice when an outburst of violent anti-Semitism in word or deed reminds them too pertinently that the days of persecution may not be past.'

These extraordinary conclusions are echoed by two other writers, again neither of whom were Austrian, who drew attention, albeit in a less ominous way, to the resentment people felt towards the Jews in Austria earlier this century. Wolf von Schierbrand, a remarkably open-minded American journalist posted in Vienna until 1916 when hostilities forced him to retire, observed how the influx of Galician Jewish refugees to Vienna in 1915 when the Eastern Front collapsed led to a severe shortage of vegetables as Jewish merchants cleared the market of these precious foods in order to sell them at a profit elsewhere. Usury also dramatically increased at this time so that, as Austrian currency became worthless, an unsavoury barter of family goods and treasures began which was to leave a bitter taste in the mouths of those families – and few were spared – who were forced to go to these Jews to trade some treasured heirloom for a pound of carrots.

Virginio Gayda, an Italian observer of the Austrians at this time, was even more scathing about the Jews and their ability to send their gentile competitors to the wall: 'Today the Jews reign in triumph in Vienna. They work little and earn a great deal; their advance is inexorable. The Catholic newspapers insult the Jews daily, but the ecclesiastical institutions, the princes and the bishops entrust their money to them for investment and speculation' (*Austria's Racial and Social Problems*, 1913).

Gayda, whose writings were stimulated by a fervent Italian patriotism and a no less passionate hatred of all things Austrian, makes Wickham Steed seem almost objective. Both, however, paint a forbidding picture of relations between Jews and non-Jews in Austria, and it is impossible to deny the prescient nature of Wickham Steed's thinking when he states: 'The danger to civilization in the Jewish question is the failure on the part of the Jews and non-Jews alike to perceive the proper difference between the Jewish and non-Jewish mentality, together with the concentration of financial and political power in Jewish hands may lead once again to those instinctive revolts of non-Jewish majorities against Jewish minorities.'

None of these foreign writers, with the possible exception of Wickham Steed, were likely to have had any influence on the Austrians' inherent anti-Semitism. There was no need, for in their Christian Socialist Mayor of Vienna, Karl Lueger, they had an anti-Semite of the most dangerous brand. This 'demagogue of genius', who from 1897 to 1910 personified the Austrian workers' stand against unbridled capitalism, recognized that the Jews were seen by the average Austrian as the agents of economic tyranny and denounced them for it. He was not, however, a Jew-hater. He paid tribute publicly to those of his friends who were Jews, though his more emotional speeches often contained the phrase for which he became famous: 'I decide who is and who is not a Jew.'

These words made it clear to the Viennese that the Jews could not be indiscriminately attacked, and that those Jews who curbed their 'immoderation' and 'ruthless malpractice' would be free to serve the empire as loyally as the next person.

Karl Lueger's reign as mayor was brief, but his language and ideas were not forgotten. As Wickham Steed noted, 'the employment of impure means to attain ends not in themselves impure entailed consequences almost as deleterious as the evils Lueger had set out to combat'. By whipping up anti-Semitism for political ends, and by the no less evil incitement of demagoguery and hysteria in a lethargic and intellectually lazy people like the Viennese, he had a far-reaching and explosive influence.

The impact of his character and politics was not lost on the nineteen-year-old house painter from Linz who found his work laughed at by architects and artists who were, in the young Hitler's eyes, hopelessly besotted with what he believed was 'Jewish art': 'I left Vienna a convinced anti-Semite,' he wrote in *Mein Kampf*.

In the 1920s, in the aftermath of the collapse of the empire, a dangerously unstable economic climate prevailed in Vienna. The aristocracy, by changing nationality from Austrian to Czech or Hungarian, had been able to hold on to some estates in the Eastern Marches, but many others were ruined. The old practice of usury continued to squeeze princes and paupers alike. There was political instability, too, which engulfed the country already fiercely divided between extreme Socialists and the Church, with every other shade of the political spectrum at loggerheads as well. There were, inevitably, Jews on both sides, and they incurred rancour from each. To the clericals they were the blood-brothers of Marx and the begetters of Communism. To the Socialists they were the gilded chariots of capitalism trampling the proletariat into the dust.

In this climate, when economic and political turmoil was fuelled by the Austrians' natural predilection towards mass hysteria, it was perhaps inevitable that the politically motivated Austrian in the late 1920s and 30s could convince himself that somewhere there were Jews conspiring to worsen his lot. The late John Lehmann, who travelled down the Danube in the 1930s, observed that the great financiers, although Austrian by nationality, were none the less almost entirely Jewish. The failure of families such as Mayr-Melnoff and Mautner-Markhof to award wage rises they had promised contributed to an atmosphere in which conversion to the anti-Semitic propaganda of National Socialism was alarmingly easy.

The controversy of the Waldheim affair has left many Europeans with an image of Austria which was unthinkable ten years ago. Instead of being seen as victims of Hitler, a harmless people given to playing violins and sitting in cafés consuming *Sachertorte*, the Austrians have become identified in the public consciousness as a race of unrepentant Nazis who seem only too eager to bring out their dusty swastikas from underneath their pillows.

Perhaps the most melancholy aspect of the Waldheim business was the complete and mutual failure of the Austrians and the rest of the world to understand each other's mentality. In the eyes of Europe and America, modern Austria was seething with unrepentant Nazis.* The Austrians, on the other hand, believed that international opinion was Jewish-dominated. Their provincial insularity did battle – and will continue to do so for some time, one fears – with a world press addicted to the spectre of Nazi atrocities.

Communications which once flowed so freely through the veins of Western cultural contacts had become poisoned in a matter of months. To many Austrians, who now have to endure frequent jibes when they travel to America on business, the late 1970s, when the Jewish Chancellor Bruno Kreisky ruled the country, must seem like a happy dream. Kreisky, for all the wrath his Socialist policies could provoke among Conservatives, was a deeply respected figure who won the admiration even of his opponents, who saw in him what every Austrian voter irrespective of political creed desires – a strong leader. He was also unique among Austrian politicians in being not only Jewish but also a representative of the old Viennese bourgeoisie, an almost extinct breed. His speeches, berating the Viennese in their own dialect, with its drawl translated into a condescending yet commanding brogue, remain for many Austrians perhaps the most memorable rhetoric to have been heard in Austrian politics since Hitler's rather different but equally commanding speeches. As a 'Persönlichkeit' (personality) he also kept at bay the subconscious Austrian need for 'a strong hand', and his presence ensured a high standard of political debate which would never have brooked the anti-Semitism of 1986.

*This seems to have culminated in an American film depicting an invasion of America by *Nazis from Waldheim's Austria*.

The Austrians' crass attitude towards the Jews and their fate in central Europe is encouraged by an almost pathological repression of unpalatable facts. It is perhaps not surprising that a country which wallowed in that apotheosis of unreality which we call the Baroque could have proved so adept at turning a blind eye to the realities of the Second World War; so adept, in fact, that it was even capable of spreading its myopic view of history beyond the frontiers of Austria.

The late Osbert Lancaster remarked that one of the most widespread and dangerous illusions is that which holds that the Austrians have always been the unwilling dupes of the callous Prussians, 'to whom all the more disagreeable phenomena of German history can be exclusively attributed' (*With an Eye to the Future*, 1967). That illusion seduced even the victorious Allies who, though aware that proportionally more Austrians had been copper-bottomed Nazis than Germans, none the less desisted from putting into action a full de-Nazification programme. The more notorious Austrians, such as Seyss-Inquart and Kaltenbrunner, were dealt with at Nuremberg (sadly Seyss-Inquart escaped the hangman's rope by committing suicide), but the hundreds who had controlled the infrastructure which enabled thousands of Austrian Jews to be carted off to the death camps were spared and allowed to return to reap the benefits of the newly created Second Republic of Austria.

It was, of course, in the Allies' interests that Austria be not too overburdened with *Angst* or guilt about its dubious role in the Reich. Many Austrians indeed had had no truck with the Nazis, and some had died heroically fighting them. It was these who represented the image the Allies most clearly wanted to see in a robust, neutral Austria which, phoenix-like, would rise from the ashes of 1945. Austria, like Czechoslovakia and Poland, became in the history books a victim of Nazi oppression rather than one of its instruments.

A small if significant crack in this image appeared in January 1985 when the Austrian defence minister, Herr

Friedhelm Frischenschlager, shook hands with a Nazi war criminal, former *Sturmbahnführer* Walter Reder, on his repatriation to Austria. Reder had been convicted of war crimes including the massacre of civilians at Marzabotto in Italy. His release, an act of charity on the part of the Italians, was crudely exploited by Herr Frischenschlager to bolster support among the right wing of his National Freedom Party, many of whose members are notoriously nostalgic about the Nazi era. These extremists are, however, only a minority of a minority party representing less than eight per cent of the electorate, sadly on the increase since 1987. They are at present no threat to Austria's democracy, though they thrive in the political atmosphere created by the resurrection of issues which have never been faced with any degree of objectivity or calm. Hysteria, an important factor in the Austrian character, emerges bubbling over into any debate which attempts to come to grips with this aspect of Austria's past.

While this state of affairs continues ignorance prevails, most disturbingly among the young, a spoilt generation brought up by parents who, having suffered extreme hardship during and after the war, now derive vicarious gratification from squandering money on their children. These precious pups are reinforced in their ignorance by an education system which is authoritarian, inflexible and perfectly designed to inculcate a young mind with useless ideas and a submissive inability to think for itself. The Austrian youth often cannot think, rationalize or, most important of all, even debate without resorting to emotions. His talents and very great hereditary gifts – for the Slav-German mixture is not without riches – are squandered in a system in which discipline, character and honesty are neglected, rotting in the debris of a society which places more value on the way a teenage boy dances than on his respect for the truth. There are few more unpalatable experiences to be had in Vienna than to visit an end-of-term school play at one of the more respected schools. The humour is heavy, the enthusiasm thin, the sparkle normally associated with the amateur painfully absent. The jokes make fun of foreigners, guest-workers and, of course, the Jews. With an educational environment like this there can be no grounds for optimism that Austria's future will prove itself any less anti-Semitic than its past.

CHAPTER IV

The aristocracy,
or a question of quarterings

*'An industrious student of the Almanach de Gotha,
I at first experienced a romantic satisfaction at
finding myself in this illustrious company but even
my starry-eyed snobbishness was not ultimately proof
against disillusionment. Of all these Maxis and
Putzis apathetically pursuing the seduction of English debs, few, I was pained to discover, displayed
the IQ of a mentally underprivileged member of the
Bullingdon or, save when exercising their professional charm, had nearly such good manners.'*

Osbert Lancaster, *With an Eye to the Future* (1967)

'Maxi', 'Putzi', 'Mucki', 'Tuschi' – it is one of the more eccentric features of what in Austria is still called the *'Erste Gesellschaft'* ('first society') that their offspring, graced with the most
distinguished and grandiose of names – Maximilian, Ferdinand, Emmanuel – are known throughout their lives by
sobriquets most Anglo-Saxons would consider too effeminate
even for their teddy bears.

This tradition, like many things to do with the Austrian
aristocracy, is an unhappy blend of snobbery and sentimentality. Only those who are related to *'Herr Graf'* (and
therefore usually *'Herr Graf'*'s themselves) can claim the
intimate contraction or the *'du'* form of address. The ubiquitous use of such nicknames conjures up an atmosphere laden
with *bonhomie* and chumminess but it belies the misanthropic
and self-centred nature which lies at the heart of the Austrian
Chapters of the *Almanach de Gotha*, the *Burke's Peerage* of the
German nobility. The days are gone when a traveller in
central Europe could observe that the Austrian nobleman

was 'generous in his patronage, discerning in his taste and humane in his conduct' (G. Kohl, *Austria*, London, 1842).

Deprived of their vast estates in Hungary, Moravia and Bohemia, the nobility have had to fall back on damp old shooting lodges in an Austria ruled by a Socialist government with little respect for the coronets of princes. The extent of their loss cannot be over-estimated. Several families lost estates the size of an English county. The Schwarzenbergs' possessions in Bohemia before the First World War were on a scale unparalleled in England since the Magna Carta. They consisted of seven *fidei* (estates) covering an area of about 45,000 acres: twelve castles, ninety-five dairies, eighty-five forests, twelve breweries, two sugar refineries, twenty-two sawmills, furnaces, graphite mines, eighty-seven churches, seventy-three parishes, 5,000 peasant families, about 1,000 workmen and 600 clerks. To quote a Dornford Yates novel set in Austria earlier this century, 'The Austrians are not like us, they're feudal.'

The loss of these lands, and with them the virtual power of life and death over the serfs who tilled their soil, perhaps explains the propensity towards melancholy which most Austrian aristocrats feel these days. What is the point of striving to achieve worldly riches when all such things, once enjoyed in so great an abundance, could be lost so easily? Their sense of dispossession is doubtless reinforced by the well-publicized hostility of the Austrian state which, after years of Socialist rule by politicians brought up on watered-down Marxist dogma, is paranoid about anything associated with the aristocracy or the monarchy.

Even the aristocrat who has kept some of his riches and preserved them from the tax man moves uneasily in this world. Forced to rent his town *Palais* to the Republic, which gives vast state banquets above his own modest quarters, he has had to take refuge in what meagre resources remain to him and, above all, in his own kith and kin. Compared to an English lord, the Austrian count's options are limited. He cannot go into politics – the most right-wing party demands an impeccable proletarian pedigree from its members – nor can he really go into business, as the state paralyses private enterprise and stifles any initiative which aims to invest capital profitably. If he wishes to serve his country, there are only two professions open to him – the army and the foreign office.

The present Austrian army is a more democratic affair than that which blundered about in the nineteenth century, though those members of the *Gotha* who are to be found among its ranks continue to blend incompetence with an even more regrettable nostalgia for the days of the German *Wehrmacht*, which in their eyes conjures up not horror but merely a brief period of success in the annals of Austrian military history.

In the diplomatic service the traditional linguistic gifts of the Austrian nobleman, when found in combination with a modest intellect, usually lead to a glittering career. The Grafs encountered here are among the most charming and agreeable of the species, enabled by dint of their profession to break out of the confines of their class and learn something of the outside world away from their families.

But the number of '*Hochwohlgeboren*' with the necessary intellectual equipment for this branch of the Austrian service, or the stoicism required for a career in the army, are inevitably few. They are far outweighed by the vast numbers who, having failed their end-of-school exams, must seek some undemanding employment in a bank, or, having succeeded in passing, can look forward to at least ten years of oversubsidized indulgence and mental rest by enrolling as a student at Vienna or Salzburg Universities.

The older generation, a marginally harder strain, prefer to concentrate on their estates where, with few exceptions, a modest income is available.

The ambition to 'rise' or make money is virtually unknown in these circles. Instead there is a lethargy that inevitably encourages insularity and introspection. Few nobilities that have survived the upheavals of the two world wars can have retained so many of the ideas of the old order. Their obsession with titles, officially banned but far more painstakingly adhered to than in England, is one manifestation of this. A haughty insistence on '*Stand*' – rank – in all matters pertaining to marriage is another.

The concept of *Stand*, feudal in its origins, nineteenth-century in its fanatical implementation, requires that partners in a marriage have an equal number of quarterings on their coats of arms or points on their coronets. In matters such as this the arbitrator is the interminable *Almanach de Gotha*, perusal of which is one of the most potent cures for insomnia known to man. A countess can be ostracized by her family for marrying a baron, while a princess who contemplates union with a commoner can be castigated for bringing shame to the name of her family. The recent marriages of the Prince of Wales and Prince Andrew are incomprehensible to the Austrian aristocracy, who cannot understand how the most successful royal family in the world can neglect the hallowed principles of *Stand*.

The deleterious effect of this unhealthy inbreeding can be seen in the physiognomies encountered at any fashionable Vienna drinks party. The young and old men have the same gait, the same voices, the same mannerisms and, of course, the same faulty mental equipment. On such occasions it is as if the entire room were filled with an arrogant, foppish crowd of halfwits all descended from a common ancestor. Anyone who stands out as different is immediately branded a leper and ignored. Foreigners fare little better, and are expected to know each other as if they were relatives. Introductions are rarely necessary among the Grafs, with the result that no effort is made to introduce even the most illustrious foreign visitors.

One princess with links to the Bulgarian royal family recently fell in love with an Englishman who, though untitled, could trace his name back to the Norman Conquest, several centuries before Her Highness's forebears had mustered a single quartering on their escutcheon. The young princess had her doubts, but, carried away by the passion of the moment and the lack of any Austrian alternative half as interesting, was prepared to risk the opprobrium that would rain upon her. But her mother, hearing that this stalwart gentleman was in town, mercilessly pursued him, taking up a position outside his rooms so as to waylay him and threaten, persuade or even bribe him to drop his suit. I am assured that this kind of behaviour is considered completely normal among Austrian families of the *Gotha*. The hapless Englishman could at least take comfort from the fact that had he been an Austrian baron he would have been no less roughly handled.

At the top of the hierarchy stand the descendants of the former ruling house, the Habsburgs, and at their head the Crown Prince Archduke Otto. The archduke, now a member of the European Parliament, has proved in that ill-starred forum of political debate that he is a man of no mean intelligence. Despite his youthful looks he is old enough to remember the funeral of the last Austrian emperor but one, Kaiser Franz Josef, in 1916. In the 1930s he was a rallying point for the monarchist movement and even offered his services to the Republic when the Nazis threatened the *Anschluss*. But, unsupported as he was by any popular following, his offer was wisely rejected by those who were more in touch with political realities. In the 1960s he relinquished his claim to the Habsburg throne so as to be allowed to return to his homeland. A few years ago his mother, the Empress Zita, who ruled for two years after Franz Josef died and has never abdicated, also returned for a brief visit. These two figures are the last impressive relics of the dynasty which once ruled the empire.

The most recent generation of Habsburgs, despite the presence of the formidable Empress Zita, whose Bourbon-Palma blood introduced a strain of psychological strength into the inbred Habsburgs' veins, has proved disappointing. Weakness and a tendency to stand on formality, refreshingly absent in the Crown Prince, is to be found in abundance among these younger scions of the family. The ease of manner, *sprezzatura* and modesty of the English aristocracy are nowhere visible among them, with the exception of those privileged few, now well into their seventies, who were packed off to Oxford before the war to study English manners and shooting. The haughtiness and ostentation of the younger set causes problems when one of them marries into the English aristocracy, where such behaviour constitutes 'bad form'. This difference of approach lies behind most of the 'difficulties' Princess Michael of Kent, the daughter of an Austrian baron, has encountered in recent years in England.

Deprived of any function in the state, and reluctant to find a new role in the modern world, the Austrian aristocracy has declined to a condition of paralysis. Indeed, they have been conditioned by history to be unfit for any other role. As Wickham Steed noted in his book *Austria–Hungary*, the Austrian aristocracy took a far smaller part in the public affairs of the Empire than the nobilities of either England or Prussia. Even during the days of the empire, the aristocrat was a 'healthy open-air being not overburdened with intellect, interested mainly in his own affairs and attributing to them greater importance than to public affairs in general . . . with few exceptions the Austrian nobleman remains a decorative rather than a useful member of society'.

That this was so was partly due to the fact that the Habsburgs in the nineteenth century rarely chose their advisers in government from the upper echelons of the nobility, preferring to rely on servants of humbler birth who, motivated by ambition, were more trustworthy than the more independently minded '*Hochadel*'. Non-aristocratic birth was no obstacle to advancement, and many were raised to the rank of count. Since all their children inherited the title, a situation arose in which nearly every second man at a ball in Vienna could claim to be a count.

The inevitable laziness which these circumstances brought about among the *Hochadel* led generation after generation to devote itself to trivia and gambling rather than more serious thought and the affairs of state. Its unyielding addiction to

Stand also encouraged this *vis inertia*, since it precluded the introduction of more vigorous blood into their veins.

Today this lassitude prevails with few exceptions, the more dynamic barons and counts coming from Jewish or Hungarian backgrounds, and the more intelligent and certainly best-mannered coming from Liechtenstein, whose princely family is well represented in Austria. The advance of Communism in Hungary after the Second World War caused a mass exodus of the landed classes from Budapest to Vienna. The Hungarian Uprising of 1956 resulted in many more Hungarians reaching Vienna, arriving penniless but within a few years recovering their lost fortunes through hard work and inspired speculation.

But these are a minority, and the visitor furnished with a few introductions to the more ancient houses will discover a class with an almost obsessive devotion to pleasure. Their enthusiasm, unlike in more northern climes, does not take the form of enjoying the sound of broken glass or indeed an excess of drink or drugs. Rather, poker-dice and reckless driving are the twin pursuits encouraged most among the over-privileged young who, though brought up to waltz well, have been woefully neglected in the less obviously glittering areas of their education.

One harmless source of amusement lies in exploiting visiting Americans' delight in sentimentality and their fascination for titles. For some years now, each summer in the Austrian capital has been marked by an extraordinary event known appropriately as the *Rosenkavalier Ball*. This annual beano, organized with great wit and efficiency by an illustrious prince well into his seventies, attempts to unite American money with impoverished Austrian nobility through the introduction of American 'débutantes' to whatever young Grafs or barons can be found in the city at a time when most of the *Erste Gesellschaft* has decamped to the Wörthersee. Great pains are taken to ensure that the most witless specimens of the Austrian titled male are assembled to escort the starry-eyed lasses from west of the Missouri, and considerable indulgence is shown towards those who, though unable to speak a word of English, are considered sufficiently impecunious to be worthy candidates. The parents of the unfortunate girls have often sunk a by no means negligible part of their family fortunes to ensure that their daughters attend this ball and the subsequent two weeks of festivities centred around the Wolfgangsee, unaware that virtually every penniless *Ritter* in Vienna is enjoying a vast dinner with limitless wine at their expense. For his part, since the *Ritter* has considerable respect for his stomach, this is an event of irresistible attraction, and a seemingly endless supply of grinning men, looking rather incongruous in formal dress, whisk the young debs off their feet, clicking heels and kissing hands in a way which affords great pleasure to simple minds. By the time the last portions of pudding have been served the majority of these chaps, bored with the company of wide-eyed sixteen-year-olds who can understand neither their language nor their lusts, melt away into the night leaving only those who have agreed, out of sheer poverty, to escort the young ladies for the next fourteen days.

In its harmless frivolity, skilful exploitation and quintessentially Austrian blend of the sentimental and the commercial, the *Rosenkavalier Ball* is one of the great high-points of the season.

Another is a ball mounted by an organization called the St Johann's Club. Its members, who are allowed reciprocal membership of such illustrious establishments as Brook's in London, are drawn from the ranks of the *Erste Gesellschaft*, with a considerable number of hangers-on who, for a small membership fee, get a chance to rub shoulders with those of sixteen quarterings. Unfortunately for them, disillusionment is swift, for the 'club' consists of only three modest rooms, none of which boasts the libraries, mirrors, leather armchairs or even newspapers associated with what the Anglo-Saxon calls a club. Furthermore, like a Fabian working-man's association, the club arranges lectures, the odd Habsburg archduke being wheeled out to discuss some arcane point of genealogical history, or drama evenings when, to the understandable and uncontrollable mirth of all present, performances of *As You Like It*, complete with Viennese waltzes, are produced to distract members for a few hours before a night at the poker table.

The St Johann's Club annual ball at first glance has most of the essential ingredients for a romantic evening: a pleasant *Schloss*, attractive countryside, adequate drink and reasonable food, though the music, predictably, is consistently appalling, relying year after year on that collective tone-deafness which is so often the mark of a society in decline. However, the disappointment of the music is nothing compared to that experienced by anyone who is unprepared for the tone of this occasion. The débutantes being Austrian, the gentlemen take tactical advantage of the surrounding parkland to introduce the young and promiscuous to the heady delights of the amorous arts. Not that this is accompanied by any element of romance, for long before the magical central European dawn arrives all the participants have raced back to Vienna for more food at one of the innumerable breakfast parties in the city.

This lack of style and complete indifference to natural beauty is no less philistine than the low esteem music and painting are held in by most younger members of the Austrian aristocracy. Faced with the choice of hearing a famous quartet play Mozart and the chance of a plate of frankfurters, I fear there can be no doubt as to which *Herr Graf* would prefer. His harrowing – to the outsider at least – ignorance and even hostility towards the arts is illustrated by the fate of one talented young English painter who, finding himself penniless in Vienna, supplemented his income by painting portraits of the younger Grafs with whom he came into contact. By the judicious addition of the relevant family escutcheon in the right-hand corner of the canvas or – in extreme cases – by painting the sitter in the full-dress uniform of the old Imperial Austrian Cavalry, he was able to guarantee his clients' satisfaction even though, as he privately admitted, most of his canvases were wretched examples of the genre and did no justice to his considerable skills as a painter.

Herr Graf's love of role-playing is seen at perhaps its most pitiful when he is *auf der jagd*. He is a fanatical huntsman who will happily spend many hours at a shooting party where shooting and only shooting can be discussed. Dressed in tweeds *à l'anglais*, his heels studded with metal and his coat cut with a crispness no English tailor would endure, he moves across the Alpine stage like a character on the losing side in a Dornford Yates novel. These shooting parties are melancholy events, combining as little exercise with as much slaughter as possible, and to those who enjoy the pace of 'walking in line' there can be no more depressing experience than sitting in a *Jagdhut* for hour after hour waiting for some unfortunate roebuck to appear and be blasted to pieces from all sides by volleys of high-powered rifle fire delivered with a recklessness that is terrifying in its intensity.

None the less, there are those who would say that it is on these occasion that the Austrian nobleman is seen at his most tolerable, and in the absence of conversation, against the background of the spectacular scenery of the Alps, it is possible to see him in a charitable light. For all his faults, he is undemanding company capable of some human warmth and considerable indulgence towards animals (when not shooting them) if not people. But even then he is all form and little substance: for more depth and character it is to the female of the species that we must turn, and that quickly if we are ever to receive an invitation to dine in a *Schloss* again.

CHAPTER V

Femme fatale:
the Austrian woman

*'The extraordinary number of good-looking women
of all classes to be seen in the streets of Vienna was
most striking, especially after Berlin where a lower
standard of feminine beauty prevailed. Particularly
noticeable were the admirable figures with which
most Austrian women are endowed.'*

Lord Frederic Hamilton,
The Vanished Pomps of Yesteryear (1919)

The young Lord Hamilton, *en poste* at the British embassy in
Vienna before the First World War, was by no means alone in
his admiration for the Austrian woman. Over the years a
reputation, reinforced by the inescapable strains of the *Kon-
gresstanz* and *Lippen Schweigen*, have embedded among the
least-travelled of Europeans the belief that Austria is a
feminine country in which women flourish unchecked, save
for the physical restraints imposed by that most feminine of
garments, the ubiquitous tight-fitting *Dirndl*. Even Edward
Crankshaw, a serious scholar and perhaps the most gifted of
all the Englishmen who have attempted to write about
Austria, could not help commenting, in his book *Vienna*
(1938), on the 'chaperoned young girls, fair, sentimental,
disarmingly cynical and with an aura of innate gaiety – with a
smile at an instant's command, a gloved hand ready to wave'.

The collective weakening of Anglo-Saxon knees in the
presence of the Austrian woman is a curious thing, no less
prevalent now than it was earlier this century if the number
of unions involving Austrian women in the Court and Social
pages of *The Times* are anything to go by. Part of the reason,
one suspects, must be the sense of relief felt when one

45

encounters an Austrian woman shortly after meeting an Austrian man. Thus Hamilton, with a true diplomat's acidic understatement: 'the great beauty of the [Austrian] girls was very noticeable, as was their height, in marked contrast to the short stature of most of the men. I have always heard that one of the first outward signs of the decadence of a race is that the girls grow taller whilst the men grow shorter.'

The height, figure and fresh-faced, healthy looks of Austrian girls have long taken their toll on the Anglo-Saxon male more accustomed to what Crankshaw referred to as the English 'plain Jane'. The greatest number of casualties perhaps were those inflicted on the British Eighth Army during their occupation of southern Austria between 1945 and 1955. One countess in particular, whose *Schloss* was an area headquarters in Carinthia, was said to have laid waste more subalterns in an Irish regiment than the combined strength of the German *Wehrmacht* in three years' campaigning.

While much has been written about the beauty and charms of Latin and French women, little has been contributed towards the study of the no less widespread and equally devastating attributes of Austrian womanhood. As in all things Austrian, it is of course to geography and history that we must turn for some clues.

I have already dwelt on the mixture of blood – Slav, Celt, Magyar and Teuton – which runs through the Austrians' veins. This explosive mixture results, as anyone who spends more than a few days in Vienna quickly sees, in some of the most grotesque manifestations of humanity to be seen anywhere in Europe. Dwarfs and men with deformed faces and limbs can be seen with a regularity evocative of the early pages of Milton's *Paradise Lost*.

There are some, simple minds from western Austria on the whole, who attribute this phenomenon to the simple fact that Vienna lies east and that a decline in human appearance inevitably accompanies all movement in that direction. This, however, is not the explanation, for anyone travelling further east will quickly note in Moravia, Slovakia and Hungary a wholesomeness among the inhabitants which is lacking in eastern Austria. Extremes of ugliness are no stranger to extremes of beauty, and the curious influences at work creating the one can equally produce the other. Thus the average Austrian girl's attractions of height and figure.

The mixture of race also affects temperament, and it is this which has perhaps exerted the most powerful fascination. For those coming from colder climes, the combination of Teuton earnestness and Slav sensuality is at first difficult to resist. The hint of cruelty which plays about Eastern eyes, evoking the violence of the Mongol hordes, combined with the softness of a Cimabue portrait, is particularly appealing. Added to this is a native coquettishness which, both playful and sincere, is invigorating to anyone more used to the far less flirtatious eyes of girls in London, where the doling out of verbal frostbite is a speciality unheard of in Central Europe.

The use of the eyes is important to the Austrian woman who, in a second, can change her seductive dreaminess to a fiery cruelty. This is a capacity found most frequently among primitive peoples well away from any urban environment (at a Scottish *ceilidh*, for example, one may observe a similar ability enjoyed by the Highlander to communicate with glances), but the small size of Austria has ensured its survival in the towns and in the only city of any dimensions, Vienna.

In Austria this formidable armoury of physical and mental weaponry is deployed for one purpose and one purpose only: that of securing a husband. Unlike in England, where so often economic and other factors intervene, marriage is a natural rather than a prudential arrangement. Emancipation in the western European sense has only penetrated the German-speaking lands as far south as Munich. East of there, Salzburg and the rest of Austria remain bastions of the old order in which a woman who has ambitions for a career is met with a combination of suspicion and hostility.

Centuries of domination by the Catholic Church have conditioned the Austrian woman to see her most important role as that of mother, and her second important role as that of wife. Antiquated procedures for divorce, coupled with the stigma the Catholic hierarchy still attaches to it, result in circumstances whereby many Austrian women, trapped in an unhappy marriage, are forced to become better mothers than they are wives.

Some women attempt to escape this fate by pursuing a career, but here they come up against formidable opposition from men, many of whom find it difficult to listen for more than a few minutes to what any woman has to say about non-domestic affairs. The concept of equality of the sexes is totally alien to the Austrian mind. Young Austrian men, spoilt silly by indulgent mothers, show no signs of breaking away from the old ideas and, consequently, manifest an almost oriental inability to perform any task traditionally associated with women. One English girl who worked as an au pair in an Austrian family was annoyed at the practical ineptitude of all the young Austrian men she encountered, who were, in her opinion, unable to execute even such simple manoeuvres as running their own baths.

This situation, though expressive of suppressed womanhood, none the less has never impeded some Austrian women from getting near to the top in fields such as journalism. In those able to battle against rather than submit to their environment it reveals a will-power and strength of character which in the Austrian context must always be seen as refreshing.

Among the Habsburgs it was often the women who showed the greater courage. Maria Theresa, in her brilliant exploitation of the Hungarian nobles at Bratislava, demonstrated the formidable qualities available to an Austrian woman bent on either ambition or revenge.

Austrian history is in fact full of the brave achievements of such women. Berta von Suttner (1843–1914), whose splendid image until quite recently adorned the 1,000-schilling bank note (now replaced with a lurid new note depicting some arcane scientist), founded an influential peace movement at the end of the last century in the face of almost insuperable opposition from her male contemporaries.

1 Ever charming, ever friendly: a happy Austrian, Dr Kurt Waldheim

4 *opposite page:* Wolfgang Amadeus Mozart, drawing by Dora Stock, 1787

5 The Vienna Musikverein: home of Austrian music and of the Vienna Philharmonic (*ÖFVW*)

6 Rainer Maria Rilke, 'a predilection towards melancholy tinged with hopelessness' a detail from a portrait in oils by Lulu Albert-Lazard, 1916

7 Austrian literature's *fin-de-siècle* seer: Karl Kraus in 1908

2 Typical product of the Austrian melting-pot: *Linienschiffsleutnant* Gottfried von Banfield, Austria's great First World War ace. His Irish origins, reinforced by Slav blood and Austrian training, produced the perfect patriot and servant of state (*Bild archiv d. Öst. Nationalbibliothek*)

3 Building a world power: Maria Theresa as a young empress

8 One Reich, one people: Hitler enters Vienna in 1938

9 Nazi ghosts haunting modern Austrian politics: 'An Austrian the world trusts'

11 Keeping Austria on an even keel:
the heir to the Habsburg claim,
Archduke Otto von Habsburg
Lothringen

10 An Austrian magnate in canine
company: Prince Karl Schwarzenberg

12 A glorious past: Austria's last
empress, Zita

13 'Of course he needs a title if he wants to marry you – he's only a baron.' Mother knows best: Romy Schneider (*Sissy*)

14 Deadlier than the male: Romy Schneider offering Austrian hospitality in *The Girl and the Commissar*

15 Smarter, tougher, the Austrian dream: Romy Schneider in *Girls in Uniform*

16 Leading from the front – that rare Austrian phenomenon, a
successful Austrian general: Archduke Charles at Aspern,
Napoleon's first defeat on land, 1809

17 Never too old to fight: Marshal Radetzky annihilates the
Italians at Novara, 1849

18 The Heldenberg, Austria's Valhalla and Radetzky's resting
place

19 'Where on earth are we?' – 'An Austrian army awfully arrayed'

20 The sound of music: Austria's crack troops take to the mountains

A similar hostility was encountered recently by Frau Freda
Meissner-Blau, an unofficial Green candidate in the 1986
presidential election. Her links with the Greens might have
led one to expect the kind of scarecrow-like figure familiar to
British television viewers from news bulletins of events at
Greenham Common. Not so: Frau Meissner-Blau, with her
dignified grey hair, resembled in many ways a figure from
imperial times, not dissimilar in looks to the mighty Berta von
Suttner herself. Yet, in spite of her perfect combination of
the forceful and motherly qualities that the Austrian male so
admires, she polled only a handful of votes and was insulted
on many occasions by Austrians whose hostility bordered on
the hysterical.

Frau Meissner-Blau was without doubt the most likeable of
all the candidates, and probably the most intelligent, but she
failed to break the rigidly defined party support of her rival
for this so-called 'non-political' post. 'She's only a woman,'
remarked the old lady on the tram, 'and she belongs at home'
– a sentiment which could be heard anywhere in Austria
during the election campaign.

The frustrations of the Austrian woman are not only confined to the sphere of politics. Even at home, if she shows too
much evidence of independence she will endanger her
chances of marriage or, if already married, threaten the
authority of her husband. Conformity is demanded at all
levels and at all times.

One young girl, a creature of enormous vitality and beauty,
suffered the most grotesque and dismissive treatment from
her suitors because she expressed a desire to run her own
business independently of any man. Her Austrian father
having married a South American beauty, she was what in
any other country would have been counted 'a stunner', but
her tall, thin appearance was considered highly unattractive
by Austrian men harbouring a deep psychological need for
the *Dirndl* figure and a more voluptuous femininity. As a
result this hapless beauty was forced to seek liaisons with
foreigners who were bewildered that such good looks could

go unappreciated in a so-called civilized country.

The more conventional Austrian girl, on the other hand, with her gifts of unspoilt femininity, uninhibited sensual nature and uncritical attitude towards men is, of course, an ideal lover. Countless Erich von Stroheim films, the plays of Arthur Schnitzler and the overture to Richard Strauss's *Rosenkavalier* leave us in no doubt on this point. The veneration of turn-of-the-century Austrian writers for the sexual expertise and passion of the Austrian working-class maid, Tibetan in its fervour, also confirms it.

But, pillow activities aside, her gifts of companionship are limited. She is, in Virginio Gayda's phrase, 'deliciously useless'. Austrian girls, he wrote at the beginning of this century, 'are beautiful, speak French very gracefully and English which is even more chic, are devoted to their capricious pleasures, and live in an atmosphere which has something unreal and unwholesome about it'. But for his out-of-date reference to the 'elegance' of Austrian 'fashions', an observation the briefest acquaintance with modern Vienna renders meaningless, his assessment is as accurate today as it was at the time.

Gayda was also struck, as must be anyone who has enjoyed some intimacy with an Austrian woman, by her remarkable blend of pride, suggestive of rank, and superstition, a survival of that primitive peasantry which once made up much of the population of central Europe and the Carpathians. It is of course the verso of that seductive mixture of cruelty and femininity that makes the Austrian woman so successful as a lover, though it remains bewildering as well as fascinating to more rational minds.

One Austrian girl, whose appearance in a *Dirndl* suggested a high degree of no-nonsense, healthy femininity, seriously believed that the English were a cold race because, England being an island, there were too many people in a confined space to allow friendship and warmth to take root. The same girl, who had studied history of art at an illustrious university for no less than nine years (though she had never heard of

Carpaccio), was equally quick to assert that anyone with blue eyes must be intellectually superior to the rest of mankind, a belief most gratifying to those of her admirers who were thus endowed, until it was discovered that this Wagnerian attitude was accompanied by the less flattering conviction that blue-eyed men also make the best house-cleaners.

The propensity of the Austrian woman for such aberrations and superstitions is, not surprisingly, conducive to neurosis, her capacity for which seems unlimited. The oppression she must endure, coupled with the richness of her gifts and the quixotic nature of her charms, is a difficult combination which in some case leads to suicide. In Vienna, where the annual number of suicides is exceeded in central and eastern Europe only in nearby Budapest, the almost daily presence of the Föhn wind in the warmer months contributes enormously to this neurosis. The late C. N. P. Powell, another perceptive writer on Austria, observed that the Föhn wind, warm and soporific in the summer, was capable of driving the strong-willed to suicide and reducing the weak-willed to madness. It is a most unpleasant aspect of life in Austria, the dry force of hot air blowing off the eastern steppes encouraging paralysis and laziness to such an extent that at its height even the pigeons will quite obliviously walk to their death beneath the traffic on the Ringstrasse.

If during the warmer months this wind encourages neurosis, the winter months, when in Vienna the knife-like wind can penetrate the thickest of overcoats, are scarcely any better. Between these two extremes are only three months of moderate weather – April, September and October. The glorious warmth of an Austrian autumn is inspiring to anyone of an artistic frame of mind, and the romanticism expressed in so many works of Austrian art and music is vindicated by this short period of time when the forces of neurosis are contained by a briefly beneficent climate. It is probably no coincidence that the number of suicides is usually at its lowest level at this time.

Austrian psychiatrists, an overworked profession living

under the shadow of the founder of modern psychoanalysis, Sigmund Freud (1856–1939), are also noticeably less busy at this time. Little has changed since the great man opened his practice in the Berggasse and was patronized by the neglected wives of the wealthy and powerful. Patients continue to be almost exclusively middle-aged females, and most cases involve a degree of melancholy induced by some minor *problème d'amour*. In the lonely hearts sections of newspapers and magazines, over which hangs an air of devastating gloom, it is predominantly women who advertise. Inevitably, perhaps, it is also among women that the highest number of suicides is reported.

Some girls, especially in what is commonly referred to as 'the media', succeed in carving out some sort of identity and career for themselves beyond the strict stereotype which imprisons most Austrian women, but even that is no guarantee of happiness. One girl, a gifted film producer whose gentle features and blonde hair were suggestive of the most feminine Austrian *Fräulein*, ceremoniously burnt her *Dirndl* and dressed for ever afterwards in men's clothes in order to dispel the rustic image which in her view put her at a severe disadvantage in a professional environment.

This mode of protest is a rarity, however, and Vienna, the most conservative city in Europe, has fewer eccentrics of this kind than have many eastern European cities. In Hungary, for example, there are far more punk girls protesting their equality than one would ever find in Austria.

Among those who are, on the other hand, perfectly happy to accept the status quo and are not easily upset by the lack of respect that goes with the nineteenth-century attitudes towards women, there is a frenzied compulsion to escape reality by resorting to promiscuity. The visitor who spends more than a few weeks in Vienna will be surprised to discover how many women over the age of forty there are who, though ostensibly happily married with children, are engaged in some kind of extra-marital relationship. The tradition of 'possessing a mistress' observed by both Wickham

Steed and Gayda has not died with the empire. Fidelity is considered a low priority among the virtues required for a satisfactory marriage, and it is no exaggeration to say that it is thanks to the stigma attached to divorce that the breaking of this marital vow is so common.

In his curious book *Europe in Zig-zags* (1928) Sisley Huddleston observed that the difference between a German and an Austrian is easily summed up by the fact that 'A German can always say no and will positively enjoy it. An Austrian never!' Possessed of more than her fair share of passions, the Austrian woman is unlikely to suffer a dull husband for long, and because her social accomplishments are so limited, she cannot fall back on the platonic pleasures which can often preserve a relationship when the physical side of things becomes problematic.

Infidelity can, however, have dangerous consequences, not least when the betrayal is discovered by the injured party. Fuses being rather short in central Europe, the resulting explosion more often than not takes the form of a violent attack. The day when one of the Austrian newspapers does not contain some harrowing tale of violence resulting from a crime of passion is yet to come. During one week of reading these depressing examples of popular journalism it is possible to read a variety of blood-curdling tales which incorporate all the possible variations on the themes of patricide, fratricide and child murder: 'MOTHER SHOOTS DAUGHTER!' ... 'FATHER STABS WIFE!' ... 'WIFE STABS DAUGHTER, SHOOTS HUSBAND AND THEN COMMITS SUICIDE!!!' – these are typical of the headlines beloved of the Austrian *boulevard Blatt*. Far from being invented to increase circulation figures among a public with an unhealthy appetite for such sanguinary tales, they are in fact only the tip of the iceberg of violent crimes investigated by the Austrian police.

The Austrian man's propensity for pseudo-*macho* behaviour, no less than the Austrian woman's capacity for infidelity, is no doubt partly to blame for this. One in ten Austrians owns a gun and, according to a recent survey

conducted by the Vienna daily *Kurier*, is 'proud of his posses-
sion'. A quarter of these weapons are pistols, and since most
of these pistols are owned by men – women preferring the
traditionally more effective if rather gruesome bread-knife
for their domestic acts of violence – the chance of being shot
by an intemperate husband is regrettably quite high. In the
course of less than three years' residence in Vienna, I have
known at least three wives who have had to hide or dispose of
their husbands' weaponry in times of crisis. In each case the
husband appeared to be the mildest of men and an unlikely
owner of a gun.

If the Austrian woman survives these trials of co-existence
unscathed she is indeed lucky, even though in other areas of
the relationship she is invariably the stronger partner, and
generally outlives her husband by several years if not
decades. That this is so is attested by the presence of vast
numbers of Austrian grannies, with a fanatical tenacity for
hanging on to life and to their possessions, who seem to
dominate life in Austria. Often they will tell you that their
husbands were killed in the war, but statistical research shows
that this is not quite true. Their aggression and intolerance,
particularly towards the young, is renowned, and any person
under the age of thirty who crosses his or her legs in a tram,
thus limiting slightly the amount of *Lebensraum* available, is
instantly rebuked, just as personal violence awaits anyone
foolish enough not to spring up instantly to offer a seat to
one of these belligerent geriatrics.

Supported by the most generous pensions to be found in
any modern Socialist country, these women grow old in a
style undreamt of by their contemporaries in other parts of
Europe. Yet this luxury, far from making them more bene-
volent towards their fellow man, instead seems to inspire
them to perpetrate petty acts of espionage against any neighbours under the age of fifty.

The young foreigner who finds himself lodged in a block
of flats full of 'jolly old ladies' is generally in for an unpleasant surprise. Any noise, however harmless, which reaches

these old ladies' ears after 9 p.m., will result in a tirade or a visit from the police who in Austria seem to spend a considerable amount of time and tax-payers' money answering summonses from disgruntled pensioners.

This behaviour goes hand in hand with an unhealthy curiosity in the details of any strangers' movements. The old traditions of Metternich's secret police die hard in Vienna, and jaundiced old ladies with too much time on their hands are the willing and enthusiastic agents of a system of surveillance which at times seems to have changed little from the days of the Third Reich.

A young English girl, on a visit to Vienna to attend a ball, returned one morning to the block of flats where she was staying and encountered an old lady who announced that she also lived in the house. The time being 6 a.m. and the English girl being attired in a ball-gown, it might be supposed that some polite inquiry into the evening's revelry might ensue. Not at all: the unfortunate girl was peremptorily asked how long she was staying and whether she was paying any money for the bed in her friend's flat. There can be no doubt that had the girl jokingly said yes, her friend would have been reported to the tax authorities within twenty-four hours.

The crushing influence that these survivors of the old order exert is one of the most potent factors contributing to the collective mental paralysis which engulfs so many of Austria's youth. There are of course exceptions, and these rare birds are of a quality that is as refreshing as it is scarce; but for the most part these old ladies represent one of the more unpleasant aspects of contemporary Austrian life and are a warning – though rarely heeded – of where marriage to an Austrian beauty can eventually lead.

CHAPTER VI

'An Austrian army awfully arrayed'

'L'Autriche a la fâcheuse habitude d'être
toujours battue.'

Talleyrand

The Austrians' reputation for inefficiency on the battlefield is a curious piece of mythology. At first glance Talleyrand's comment seems to have a pithy truth about it, for almost every campaign the Austrians waged in the nineteenth century ended in military disaster. Yet at least three Austrian generals stand comparison with the greatest military leaders in the world, and the quality of Austrian soldiery was held in considerable esteem by many nineteenth-century observers. Thus Wickham Steed in 1913: 'of the excellent fighting qualities of the Austrian soldier it is superfluous to speak. They have been shown on a hundred battlefields.'

The modern visitor to Austria will find little evidence of this proud ancestry among the present Austrian army. In Vienna, where a guard battalion performs ceremonial duties outside the Hofburg when ambassadors present their credentials to the president, there is no suggestion in either their appearance or drill that the great traditions of the Imperial and Royal Army are taken seriously. The drill is sloppy, the uniforms both impractical and ugly, and, were it not for the painted white lines on the tarmac in front of the president's chancery entrance, it is doubtful whether the formations would ever manage the feat of standing in a straight line.

In the early days of the empire the Habsburgs were capable of waging war as effectively as any of their European rivals, though they preferred to add to their possessions by the more peaceful expedient of dynastic marriages. In the seventeenth century western Europe, when threatened by the Infidel, looked to Austria to act as the bulwark of Christendom, and in the brilliant series of campaigns which forced the Turks back to Belgrade, Austrian soldiery won its spurs on a scale that proved they were capable of far more than the local engagements which marked the Thirty Years War earlier in the century. The victories which culminated in the Battle of Zenta and the Peace of Carlowitz in 1699 gave the Habsburgs not only all of Hungary but also Croatia, Slavonia and Transylvania.

To fight against the Turk, who rarely gave any quarter, was a test of courage as well as endurance. However, victory cannot be won by first-class soldiery alone, and that this campaign was a success was largely also due to the fact that at their head the Austrians had Prince Eugène of Savoy. Though not an Austrian (Eugène was a member of the collateral branch of the House of Savoy), this hunchback prince, whose ugliness was the talking-point of the court gossips, was, like the Irish generals Nugent, O'Donnell and Kray and the Italian Montecucuoli, one in a long line of foreign military servants of the Habsburgs whose names became intimately associated with the Austrian army.

It may perhaps come as a surprise to many British readers that the celebrated Battle of Blenheim was as much Eugène's victory as it was the Duke of Marlborough's. It was Eugène whose idea it was that Marlborough make the dramatic march to the Danube from the Rhine and so effect the junction with the Austrians which was to have such disastrous consequences for the French. It was also Eugène who at the height of the battle saved Marlborough's life by detailing a group of cavalry to the duke's aid when he was in peril and the British centre seemed about to collapse.

Eugène was perhaps guilty of lacking precision in detail, but for rapidity of vision he had no equal. He was able to sum up a situation within seconds and improvise to solve the essential point of any strategic problem. In temperament he was the opposite of his ally Marlborough, though the two men enjoyed each other's respect and friendship despite their very different approaches. This difference is perhaps best illustrated by the tale of how, at Blenheim, the duke, seeing some of his cavalry riding away from the action, drily observed: 'Gentlemen, the enemy lies that way.' A few minutes later, at another part of the battlefield, the prince, seeing some of his infantry falter, promptly shot two men who turned to run away from the enemy. (It is equally typical of Prince Eugène to have had many of his favourite treatises on war bound in the skins of the janissaries he had defeated on his Turkish campaigns.)

By the end of the first decade of the eighteenth century, Austrian feats of arms had earned a reputation which was not to be treated lightly. But four years after Prince Eugène's death in 1736, the accession of Maria Theresa led to a military confrontation which destroyed that reputation at a stroke. The War of the Austrian Succession (1740–48) first introduced the world to the Habsburg army's capacity for disaster.

When Breslau in Silesia was under threat from the Prussians, the Austrian high command did nothing, and actually prohibited one relief force from going to Breslau's aid as the danger was not considered acute enough at court. Eventually Maria Theresa found some generals she could rely on: Daun, Laudon and Khevenhuller each gave Frederick the Great something of a run for his money, and had they been up against a less brilliant tactician they would have fared with rather more success than they did. But what is of interest to the student of the Austrian character here is not that the Austrians were so decisively and repeatedly defeated but that on several occasions, such as Breslau, their almost frivolous indifference enabled a more determined opponent to take advantage of them.

Military history records few episodes more curious than the Battle of Torgau (1760) in which the Austrians were commanded by Leopold Daun. Daun had shattered the myth of Prussian invincibility in 1757 at the Battle of Kolin and defeated them again two years later, with Russian help, at Kunersdorf, but at Torgau his behaviour was what might be described as extravagantly Austrian. In what looked like a decisive victory for the Austrians, their Croat battalions had driven the Prussians off the battlefield and sent them into so obvious a retreat that Daun ordered his own reserves to withdraw. Pickets were placed on the hills, and by 4 p.m. dispatch riders had been sent to Vienna to tell the empress of a great victory. The pickets, also Croats, engaged in a fit of plundering, raiding all the farmhouses for anything edible with which to celebrate. The Prussians, observing the withdrawal of Daun's main force, promptly reformed and returned to give battle. Within an hour the entire Austrian force had been routed, and a new dispatch had to be hurriedly sent to Vienna.

There is, to anyone who has studied the Austrian mind, something undeniably typical about this incident. The initial strategy had been sound, the troops and their officers had fought bravely and doggedly, and then, with complete victory within their grasp, the entire winnings had been thrown away on a fatal assumption that their opponents' lethargy would be as great as their own.

This failure to follow through is a recurring feature of Austrian campaigns. Forty years later it was to manifest itself most spectacularly in the five wars they waged on Napoleon. The tenacity of the Austrians during these bleak years is remarkable. Five times between 1790 and 1813 a new army was trained and marched off to do battle, only to return four time in varying stages of annihilation. The tables were finally turned at Leipzig, with Russian help, but the battle which is more significant is that of Aspern in 1809, when an Austrian army, led by the Archduke Charles, inflicted on Napoleon his first-ever setback on land. But again, it was failure to follow through their initial success which led to a catastrophic defeat a few week later at the Battle of Wagram. After two days of carnage, Napoleon was able to bring up superior forces to outnumber the Austrians, who tenaciously held on for relief by a force under Archduke Johann which, when it materialized, was too late to affect the outcome. The Emperor Francis I, looking impeturbably on at this bloodiest of Napoleonic contests, remarked with an indifference born of ruthlessness: 'I think it's time we were getting home.'

The campaign of Aspern–Essling–Wagram has received scant attention from historians, but even the most superficial examination of the events of those days is enough to discount any aspersions cast on the mettle of Austrian soldiery. Archduke Charles, who with Prince Eugène must be considered one of the great generals of Austrian military history, failed partly because of his whimsical over-confidence and partly as a result of his proneness to fits of epilepsy, a disease hereditary in the Habsburgs.

Though Austria acquitted herself honourably towards the end of the Napoleonic Wars, for the rest of the nineteenth century her performance was patchy. Only in 1848, in the campaign against Italy, did a combination of gifted generalship and brave soldiery emerge again to win a minor war.

It remains one of the great ironies of this campaign that its hero was a general in his eighty-third year who commanded less than 50,000 troops against forces superior in numbers and equipment. Marshal Radetzky (1776–1858), who is perhaps best remembered for the rousing Strauss march he inspired, was an eccentric figure devoted, like every true Austrian soldier, to women and gambling, but he had a sound grasp of tactics which makes his 1848 campaign one of the great set-pieces for study in military history classes throughout the world.

Marshal Radetzky is also remarkable for having inspired one of the most extraordinary monuments ever erected in honour of a military hero, a monument which offers a curious insight into the Austrian attitude to feats of arms. By the time he was in his mid-eighties the marshal, as a result of his addiction to high living, was heavily in debt. A certain Josef

Parkfried, a tin merchant of some wealth, having secured the contract to supply this metal to the Imperial Army, offered to pay all the marshal's debts in return for his body which he proposed, on the hero's demise, to bury at the centre of a shrine commemorating Austria's military success during the 1848 insurrection. The marshal agreed, and thus began a few years later the construction of the most grotesque Valhalla ever contemplated, at Kleinwetzdorf in Lower Austria. Around the tomb, on which was emblazoned the belligerent warning 'Just because we are silent it does not mean we are dead', a group of 150 tin busts representing the generals, officers and even privates who distinguished themselves in 1848 was arranged along a series of symmetrical paths. Life-size knights in suits of armour surround this assembly, and in the nearby woods several vestal virgins, again executed in tin, gaze dreamily up to the summit of the hill.

The entire creation, littered with hallmarks of the *opera buffa* so conspicuously absent from Prussian military monuments, defies serious reaction from the modern spectator, and I imagine many of the foreigners who visited it after it was completed in the 1860s would have found it a comic rather than dramatic experience. But Parkfried's efforts, however eccentric, emphasize an important point: in Austria the army was loved but not respected, the exact reverse of the situation in Prussia.

It would be wrong to leave 1848 and the Radetzky Heldenberg without reference to the unsavoury figure of General Haynau. Haynau has the dubious distinction of being what might be termed modern history's first war criminal. In comparison with the wars of the eighteenth century, the battles of the nineteenth century were affairs of vast carnage on a scale hitherto unheard of. This doubtless hardened many soldiers and officers into a mode of behaviour increasingly callous of civilian life, but Haynau during his brief activity in Hungary and Italy went far beyond such limited barbarism when, to the horror of the civilized world including the court in

Vienna, he ordered the flogging in public of women and children.

Despite such atrocities Haynau, though almost immediately transferred from his command, continued to enjoy the respect of many Austrians, who in the nineteenth century were just as adept at turning a blind eye to what they did not want to see as they are now. His statue adorns one of the niches of the 'Hall of Heroes' in Vienna's spectacular military museum, and there is little in the old history books of Austria to suggest that he distinguished himself so ignobly in 1848. (It is well known in England but unfamiliar in Austria, even to many serious students of history, that Haynau, on a visit to London, was thrown into a barrel of ale by English workmen at a brewery who were incensed that the 'Hyena Haynau' was on the premises.)

The remainder of the nineteenth century was marked by a now characteristic lethargy in two great campaigns involving Austrian forces, first in 1859 against a Franco-Italian force and then seven years later in 1866 against the best-equipped and most powerful army on the continent – the Prussian.

During the Franco-Austrian War the Austrians advanced triumphantly into Piedmont but then, despite being within striking distance of Turin, wasted three precious weeks in inactivity. This allowed the French to pour in troops who sent Austria reeling at Magenta and then later at Solferino where, to the consternation of many, no use was made of the superb Austrian cavalry division on the left wing.

The lack of cohesion between commanders and the mediocre quality of generalship in this war was to have far-reaching political – as well as military – effects a few years later at the Battle of Königgratz, when Prussia ousted Austria as leader of the German states. In a bloody contest which spectacularly revealed the neglect and lack of seriousness from which Austrian military science suffered, Austrian frontal attacks with bayonets, last used with any success a generation before, were devastated by volleys from Prussian breach-loaders. The appalling discrepancy in weaponry, resulting in losses over twice as high among the Austrians as among their opponents, was matched by the near-insane behaviour of the Archduke Leopold who, despite express instructions to break off his action against the Prussian advance guard and fall back to a stronger position, called back a brigade and proceeded to attempt to dislodge a handful of Prussians from a forest. The first battalion which attempted this was decimated, but the other regiments, far from learning from this *folie de grandeur*, proceeded to charge down into the plain which promptly became the scene of a massacre. In less than two hours over one third of the archduke's forces had been disabled.

This act of indiscipline was echoed a few hours later when two corps under the command of Counts Festetics and Thun disobeyed their commander-in-chief's orders and squandered themselves in theatrical frontal charges in an attempt to destroy another numerically inferior force of Prussians, again well protected in a forest. At this rate the battle was soon over and the Austrians, routed so totally, lost some 44,000 men against the Prussians' 9,000.

Königgratz must rank as one of the most catastrophic defeats ever experienced by an army. The commander-in-chief of the Austrian forces involved, Benedek, was unjustly held to blame for the disaster: this humble, earnest and heroic soldier had in fact been consistently let down by his aristocratic corps commanders who expended regiments like chips on a roulette table. Military history knows few more shameful chapters than the Habsburgs' acquiescence in the witch-hunt which ensued against Benedek. No criticism or whiff of scandal could touch the competence of the Habsburg commanders involved, and Benedek was forced to endure all criticism himself. He did this silently, without protest, but when he died in Graz he gave orders that he would not be buried in his uniform, as Austrian military tradition demanded, a gesture which fully expressed his contempt for those he had striven to serve so faithfully.

The lessons of Königgratz, in particular the need for more

modern equipment, were learned, and the Austrian army became a more efficient engine of war than that which had gone to battle against the Prussians in 1866. The uniforms were changed from the impractical though elegant white to various shades of blue. The great artillery factories of Bohemia began producing impressive guns, forerunners of the howitzers which demolished the French and Belgian defences in a few days in 1914. But the return fight against Prussia never materialized and over fifty years were to pass before the Habsburgs needed to mobilize their army fully again.

By the time the fateful year 1914 arrived, the reforms of the 1870s were themselves now out of date and Austria-Hungary found herself engaged in a war on three fronts for which she was poorly prepared. Like the French, the Austrians went into this Armageddon dressed in scarlet and blue. The cavalry officers, ever dreaming of a great equestrian conflict, yearned for a chance to pit their lances against the Cossacks' sabres, but a few weeks campaigning in the Carpathians revealed all too clearly the effectiveness of the machine-gun, which would often be deviously mounted behind squadrons of cavalry which, after encouraging the Austrian cavalry to charge, would wheel out to left and right leaving the riders to face a hail of bullets.

The skill with which the Austrians extricated themselves, with German help, from one emergency after another during the following four years did them credit. Their native gift for improvisation was as valuable in war as it was in peace, and in these circumstances its relationship with the art of survival became particularly intimate. This gift was especially useful in an army made up of twenty nationalities and welded into a whole by a code of only sixty-seven German words of command. This polyglot force survived intact for a remarkably long period of time – right up until the last week of the war – before disintegrating into the separate nationalities which found themselves forming with the end of the Habsburg empire.

21 *'Felix Austria'*: Bruno Kreisky, Austria's former chancellor in rhetorical flow in the Parliament

22 Taking politics seriously: conservative Austrian students toasting the past

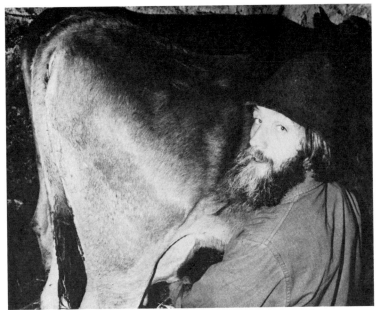

23 Milking Austria's scandals: Green politician Caspanaze Sima holding a press conference in Vorarlberg

24 Charisma is all: Jörg Haider, leader of the right-wing Freedom Party and Austria's most persuasive politician

25 Sweet and filling: Salzburg's
mouth-watering pudding, the
Salzburger Nockerl

26 Naughty but nice! Cakes at
Demel's

27 The café: Vienna's contribution to civilization. The Café Prückel.

28 The vineyards of Burgenland: Rust, flagship of Austria's wine trade

29 Where the best German is spoken: the Burgtheater in Vienna

30 Towering, unrivalled St Stephen's cathedral

31 Building the Ringstrasse: the Josefstadt in 1860

32 Salzburg: Alpine Austria's choicest jewel

33 The tomb of the Emperor Maximilian, Innsbruck

34 Sleepy southern Austria: Graz, the country's second largest city

35 'In the mountains, there you feel free'

36 Tyrolean charm: Innsbruck

The feeling of desolation and bitterness this collapse engendered in Austria affected the army more acutely than civilians. The holding of the Italian front, the rolling back of the Romanian and the drubbing they had given the Russians left many Austrian soldiers with a burning conviction that they had lost the war through no real fault of their own.

Not surprisingly, this was a rich soil in which to plant the seeds of revenge, and it is often overlooked that the next war was in many ways an attempt to set the clock back to 1914. On many fronts during the Second World War this is literally what happened, as Professor D. Rusinow relates in his book *Italy's Austrian Heritage, 1919–46* (1969). In the northern provinces of Italy and Yugoslavia, formerly ruled by the Austrians, many officers returned to take up positions they had occupied as subalterns twenty years earlier.

The performance of the Austrian divisions of the German *Wehrmacht*, a military force which must rank as one of the most efficient armies ever mobilized, was rarely inferior to that of the Prussians, and it is one of the more disagreeable features of modern Austria that where nostalgia is encountered among Austrian soldiers it is invariably for the battles of the Third Reich rather than those of the Habsburg empire. These regrettable feelings are perhaps best illustrated by the erection in 1986 of a memorial tablet in the Austrian Military Academy to General Löhr, the commander of the *Wehrmacht* Army Group E who was also an ace in the Austrian air force in the First World War. There might at first glance seem nothing wrong in commemorating an officer who had distinguished himself in both world wars, but Löhr was executed as a war criminal in Belgrade in 1947 for having personally ordered barbarous reprisals against Yugoslav civilians.

It is a curious, rather dangerous, and typically Austrian characteristic to extol the virtues of this man while burying his crimes in a morass of disinformation. After a stiff protest from the Yugoslav government the tablet was removed, not, significantly, by the Ministry of Defence which had erected it but by the Ministry of Construction, which to its embarrassment had to perform a task the Defence Minister, fearful of offending right-wing sensibilities, shirked.

Today's Austrian army, a well-equipped conscript force, is unlikely to see battle to prove its competence, but it will remain an unwholesome institution as long as a proportion of its officers remain wedded to the idea that the only Austrian army worth taking seriously was that which fought under Adolf Hitler.

CHAPTER VII

Government by administration

'There is not government in Austria. Only tyranny
softened by incompetence.'
Viktor Adler, father of Austrian Socialism

While it would be unfair to apply Adler's comment, directed
at the Habsburgs in the early years of this century, to the
present system of government in Austria, it cannot be denied
that more than a vestige of tyranny has survived in the vast
army of bureaucrats which still governs every detail of the
Austrian's day-to-day existence. Established in the reign of
Maria Theresa to administer the far-flung territories of the
empire, it retains considerable executive power, consumes
equally considerable public revenues, and in comparison with
other European countries employs a disproportionate per-
centage of the population.

The Austrian *Beamte* or civil servant enjoys a position completely different from that of civil servants in England. As a
member of a privileged class, receiving pensions and other
benefits that his counterparts in other countries would envy,
he sees himself not as a servant of the public, in the British
sense, but as the embodiment of the state, and he will not
hesitate to invoke its immense powers of obstruction if he
feels its authority ignored or its importance questioned.

This attitude of unchallengeable superiority over those he
administers encourages both a dislike of responsibility and a
tendency to cloak his administrative functions in procedures,
elaborated by the practice of generations, which at best can
be called elusive. The foreign correspondent who urgently
needs a report on the progress of an application to demolish
a beautiful garden, or the opinion of a minister on a vital

affair of state, is knocked like a ping-pong ball from one office to another. Dr X pleads that it comes under the jurisdiction of *Herr Hofrat* Y ('*Hofrat*', or court councillor, is the most prestigious, if absurd, title in Austria) who, when tracked down many hours later between a coffee break and a luncheon appointment, exclaims, 'Me, Sir? Why, surely you must talk to my old friend Dr X.' And so the game begins, giving one the inescapable feeling that however many squares one covers one is never really going to get beyond GO.

This time-wasting pursuit, magnified a hundred times, gives some indication of the workings of the '*Beamtenstaat*', in the face of which the most persistent investigative journalist becomes demoralized and the most forward of lobbyists is deflected. Even the foreigner who spends only a few weeks in the country will come into contact with these privileged drones alarmingly easily. His radio must be licensed; his flat will often be rented from an administration (*Haus Verwaltung*) rather than a private owner; he must register with the police; and so on. To the northern visitor accustomed to the impersonal, business-like approach of such bodies in other European countries it must be a source of constant bewilderment as to how the ordinary Austrian survives.

The answer is quickly discovered. Few words have a more unpleasant ring to them, and are used more frequently in Austria, than '*Protektion*'. This one word is the Austrian's guardian angel and his help in all troubles. With *Protektion* anything can be achieved with the minimum of time and expense; without it, a truly Kafkaesque fate awaits the citizen.

The political parties offer the easiest and most accessible way of obtaining *Protektion*. Since the establishment of the Second Republic in 1955, each of the three main parties – the Socialists, the conservative People's Party and the nationalist, right-wing Freedom Party – is allowed to appoint its own servants to each ministry. Therefore, in return for party membership, certain favours, and by this I mean a minimum of obstruction, can be brought into play to ease one's way through the administrative nightmare. A few examples should suffice to illustrate this.

Herr W arrives in Vienna and must register with the police. The relevant department occupies a forbidding building not far from the Danube Canal. He must bring with him photographs, papers, certificates of employment, etc., but above all he must be prepared to wait and pace the crowded corridors before being allowed into the small room where the walls are taken up with shelf upon shelf of street names and house numbers. Then he will be shouted at and generally treated with a mixture of contempt and arrogance until the business is concluded. If, however, his papers are not in order, this treatment will be repeated at regular intervals over the following weeks. It matters little to the officials that the visitor may have little time to spare or that he may have an appointment with the chancellor himself that same morning; the bureaucracy must take its course.

If, however, Herr W belongs to a party or, by virtue of his job, he enjoys a certain amount of *Protektion* through, for example, his capacity to inflict harm on Austria's public image, an altogether more agreeable fate awaits him. On announcing his credentials to someone who understands his position, he will be immediately put in touch with *Hofrat* X of a police department in an altogether more salubrious part of town. He arrives there, shows his papers, and in five minutes, without needing to wait for a moment in the corridor, is able to leave, his affairs completely in order, his impression of the Austrian authorities as kindly, well-mannered officials confirmed.

Another example: a parcel arrives through the post, a present from a relation, a few books, a shirt, some chocolates. Nothing is over the value of £25, but before the parcel can be picked up from the post office, taxes amounting to £18 must be paid. The unfortunate recipient who questions this is allowed the opportunity to present his case at the main customs depot should he so wish to. This is miles away from the post office and consists of a long building not unlike an airship shed along one side of which runs a series of about eighty desks each manned by a bored-looking man in overalls languidly contemplating an immense pile of parcels. When after a few hours the recipient's name is called out he can remonstrate and have the parcel opened to show that the goods are indeed worth only £25 and so the taxes can be slightly reduced. However, the time consumed in this expedition may leave one wondering whether the saving justified the effort.

An entirely different set of circumstances applies in the case of a recipient who, perhaps through membership of a political party or business, has access to a member of the Finance Ministry which is ultimately responsible for all customs matters. The briefest of phone-calls is all that is usually necessary to ensure effective action. The recipient must still visit the airship hangar, but instead of waiting he is shown by the man at the relevant desk to a small room where the parcel is fished out and after a few moments declared to be taxable at only half the amount originally requested. If this still proves too much, and the recipient suggests that it be sent back to wherever it came from, an amusing situation develops. The parcel inspector and his colleague huddle in a corner deep in *sotto-voce* conversation, looking worried. They then return and the amount is halved again, an offer so Balkan in its manner that it usually proves irresistible. The comic climax is still to come however, for when the parcel is finally surrendered, the green customs form declaring the goods value on the envelope has been changed from £25 to £15.

This off-stage *opera buffa* leaves the recipient in no doubt that the parcel man at desk 56 is no less free of bureaucratic constraint than anyone else. Clearly the need to satisfy the visitor transcended all the rules, and one can only guess what fate would have ensued had the recipient gone away dissatisfied and voiced his grumbles to his 'friend' at the Finance Ministry.

Multiply these experiences a thousandfold in a year and it

becomes clear that *Protektion* is the most important thing in an Austrian's life. His job, his chances of promotion, his house, his children's education – all can be subject to the vagaries of this system of mutual assistance and back-scratching. Favours received mean favours returned; ability, tenacity and talent are all relegated to a lowly position.

In no place is this more true than in the Austrian Parliament. The building itself is one of the least obviously impressive on the Ringstrasse. Its neo-classical columns are completely dominated by the more bombastic towers and fortress-like battlements of the Town Hall next door. An anarchist, should his inclination lie towards pyrotechnics, could walk right up to the Parliament building and place his explosives undetected at the main gates. Were he to try this at the Town Hall he would doubtless be restrained by one of the specially uniformed Town Hall guards who vigilantly patrol every entrance. The reason for this discrepancy is obvious once one has been in both of these buildings. Whereas the Town Hall is bustling with activity, with burghers entering with queries or problems every hour, the Parliament seems invariably empty, with the air of a grand mausoleum, except during formal occasions like the swearing in of the new government or president; its long classical corridors reverberate to few footsteps, and there is about the entire building a hush which could persuade the impressionable who first enter it that they are in a museum rather than the power-house of Austrian democracy.

The absence of any obvious activity on the part of Austria's parliamentarians is even more evident in their debates. Few of these are ever covered by the Austrian press, which rightly perceives their irrelevance to the country's affairs, and there is no parliamentary page in the Vienna papers. The cut and thrust of rhetorical challenges never rings out over the debating chamber of the body which with Austrian irony is called 'Hohes Haus'.

I well remember one of the few debates to attract the interest of the media in recent years. A motion of no confidence was proposed by the opposition in the wake of the Austrian Defence Minister Herr Friedhelm Frischenschlager's crass handshake with a war criminal on his repatriation to Austria (see p. 32). The chancellor, Dr Fred Sinowatz, read his opening speech at breathtaking speed, which underlined his obvious lack of enthusiasm for parliamentary debate. The voting had all been decided before: the government would stand behind its minister rather than concede a point to the opposition. During the interminable speeches that followed, each politician was applauded consistently and with clockwork precision. Any parliamentarian who noticed the lack of spontaneity, dignity and eloquence displayed on this occasion must have longed for the scathing tirades of the former chancellor, Bruno Kreisky, who virtually single-handedly raised the standards of political debate here during the 1970s.

The extent of Kreisky's achievement cannot be underestimated for, unlike the Hungarian Parliament, which throughout the later part of the nineteenth century boasted a fine tradition of rhetoric and political debate, Vienna's Parliament was always something of a circus. The dispatches of the *Times* correspondents in the 1880s and 90s give a picturesque view of proceedings. Had these reports not been preceded by headlines such as 'VIOLENT SCENES IN THE AUSTRIAN PARLIAMENT', they could have been mistaken for one of the paper's drama reviews of a music hall. Hunting horns were frequently blown, a variety of other musical instruments were often brought in to disrupt speeches that were too relevant, and acts of personal violence were a regular occurrence.

When the Habsburg Empire collapsed, the First Austrian Republic was therefore unable to rely on a sound parliamentary tradition, and the breakdown of this fragile institution soon followed, leading to a brief but bloody civil war in 1934 and the complete suppression of Parliament by the clerical-Fascist Chancellor Engelbert Dollfuss. The present Parliament, dating from the beginning of the Second Republic in 1955, is thus still in its infancy, and for this reason perhaps should merit some sympathy. However, it will remain impossible to take the Austrian political system seriously as long as the bureaucracy continues to exert so much influence and the decision-making process operates behind the scenes rather than on any political stage.

The Frischenschlager debate demonstrated several unfortunate symptoms of the lack of maturity Austrian democracy still labours under. A minister belonging to the right-wing Freedom Party had personally welcomed a convicted Nazi war criminal, had brought dishonour and international outrage upon his country, and in the ensuing furore had done nothing to atone for this 'mistake' beyond saying merely that he was sorry. He did not offer to resign, nor did he, after admitting his error, see the logical necessity to dissociate himself from the Socialist majority of ministers in the government which so abhorred his action.

This spineless behaviour and pathetic fear of taking responsibility for a misdeed, coupled with an almost adolescent belief that by saying sorry all will be well, vividly exposes the disease that afflicts the Austrian democratic process. Part of the reason why the minister did not resign was because as an individual he, like every other minister in Austria, has no real say in such matters. He owed his position as minister not to any ability or talent but to *Protektion*, in this case his party. His party had enabled him to rise to the heights of his profession. His party – and only his party – could allow him to descend from these heights.*

Had the Freedom Party not been so keen to avoid offending its extreme right-wing minority of supporters the minister might conceivably have tried to resign, but as it was, he had to remain, and the disgruntled Socialists, rather than risk losing the Freedom Party's support in Parliament, had to support him.

*The hapless Herr Frischenschlager was quietly removed as Defence Minister over a year later, but as he was promoted to leader of the parliamentary Freedom Party it would seem that his 'mistake' has not impeded his career.

When, however, a party is determined that a blunder has taken place which, though infinitely more trivial than Herr Frischenschlager's foolishness, demands retribution it will mercilessly force the minister to resign. Herr Karl Sekanina, the Minister for Construction, was believed, thanks to a curious press campaign which pursued its victim mercilessly on nothing more than circumstantial evidence, to have appropriated trade union funds to finance his villa in Vienna. He may have been innocent, but no quarter was given to him and his resignation, though forced upon him, was subsequently held up as an example of how the concept of ministerial responsibility thrives in Austria's democracy!

The three main parties, like the civil service bureaucracy, typify the inertia of modern Austrian political life. The Socialists, who have held power now for almost two decades, are still the 'red' party of the workers – referred to with alarming regularity by many Austrians as the 'proletariat'. Not since its heroic beginnings under the aegis of Viktor Adler (1852–1918) and his followers has it managed to renew its philosophy with changing political realities. Its rhetoric is an unhappy and unreal blend of diluted Marxism and shameless materialism. It has decayed in power, complacent and smug, seemingly unaware that there is no longer a class struggle in Austria, that there is no such thing as an impoverished proletariat, and that Austrian workers now enjoy a style of life which in any other Western country would be perceived as middle class.

The formality and fear of change which the Socialist Party suffers from has made it increasingly intolerant. The celebrated party paper, the *Arbeiter Zeitung*, was turned into a tabloid and moved out of its prestigious art deco offices along the Wienzeile partly because its repeated calls for reform had irked the older fathers of a party unwilling to enter into a straightforward debate on the future of Austrian Socialism. The party is so laden with dead wood, and so lacking in dynamism and the will to identify the problems of the future, that any young man or woman with political ambition can only turn elsewhere for opportunity. The emergence in recent months of Chancellor Vranitzky has, however, stopped the rot, and the party may revive.

Failure with the young has been the one error of the Socialists which has not been repeated by its principal rival, the Austrian People's Party, which has gone to great lengths to woo the conservative young Austrian. This party, which is referred to as the 'Black' party on account of its clerical origins, has traditionally been the voice of the Catholic rural provinces diametrically opposed to the Socialists in Vienna and other cities. In theory it represents the professional classes, standing for a more entrepreneurial economy and against excessive public spending. In practice there is not a single policy which the People's Party can offer that differs in any radical way from the ideas of the Socialists.

A political party that has no ideological axe to grind and no interests other than a naked desire for power clearly cannot attract the best minds. Many People's Party politicians stand at elections not because they believe in the intellectual or philosophical superiority of their approach but simply because they want and need the power that can be exercised through the victorious party's ability to control the ministries. Besides, the generous remuneration and privileges such as free electricity and travel subsidies which the Austrian Member of Parliament enjoys are considered enough reward for most who contemplate a career in public life.

The third and smallest of the main political parties, the so-called Freedom or 'Blue' Party, is something of an exception. While it does not openly profess any radical alternative to the policies of the two main parties, it none the less harbours sentiments which are blatantly nationalistic and radically right-wing. In Carinthia, where there is a Slovene minority around the town of Klagenfurt, the most popular politician is the Freedom Party's firebrand Jörg Haider, elected leader of the party in November 1986. He makes no secret of his German nationalist sentiments and openly calls for the establishment of separate Slovene and German schools, a move which would satisfy the demands of many right-wing German Carinthians who loathe the idea of their children sharing a classroom with Slavs whose mother tongue is not German.

The roots of the Freedom Party lie in the old Austrian Liberal Party, which in the days of the polyglot Habsburg empire was virulently anti-Slav. Unlike the Liberal Party in England, it was always on the right wing of the political spectrum. When it was formed after the last war, it attracted many former Nazis who despised both the Socialists and the Catholic People's Party, and the Austrian political scene has been rocked more than once by controversy surrounding the dubious past of some of them. Although it can be supposed that they will eventually die off, if the career of the young Herr Frischenschlager is anything to go by the shining post-war image of the Freedom Party is just as misguided as the old.

It should, however, be emphasized that the Freedom Party's prestige and power have been grossly exaggerated by its recent period of coalition with the Socialists. Its support, marginally less than eight per cent of the electorate, is mainly confined to the province of Carinthia where two invasions this century by Slavs, following the two world wars, have left the German Carinthians with a distinct Slavophobia.

With these three parties to choose from, until two or three years ago it was impossible for radical Austrians to find any politician to support with any real conviction. Apathy with the way Austria was governed in the years after Kreisky's resignation in 1983 reached a peak of resentment in the winter of 1984–5 when his successor, Dr Fred Sinowatz, attempted to clear a celebrated unofficial nature reserve near the Czech border not far from the medieval village of Hainburg in order to erect a hydro-electric power station. In what was the first spontaneous mass public demonstration against the government in the history of the Second Republic, thousands of Austrians ranging from punk rockers to ageing countesses occupied the swamp and Auwald forests of the threatened area in sub-zero temperatures to prevent it being cleared. The government panicked and sent in the police, but after repeated scenes of violence unparalleled in the country's recent history, the chancellor was forced to back down and cancel the project. Overnight, idealism clad in the rubber boots and anoraks of the Greens had come to impart some energy and direction into the lacklustre and bewildered Austrian political stage.

A few months earlier, the Greens had scored a notable success during local elections in the country's westernmost province of Vorarlberg, which resulted in the seating of the provincial parliament having to be reorganized to accommodate the new party. Polls predicted that in a general election they could capture as much as thirty-six per cent of the vote, while journalists trekked out to a remote Alpine valley to interview one of the Greens' eccentric leaders, Caspanaze Sima. Herr Sima, whose maiden political speech was unintelligible to all who did not have a sound grasp of Vorarlberg dialect, was fond of entertaining these journalists with a demonstration of the rustic art of milking cows. He represented to the young idealist Austrian a unique departure from the typical Austrian politician. He was motivated neither by lust for power nor greed for material wealth but simply by a desire to improve the quality of life in his country. Needless to say, what has been achieved in the provinces of Austria will be difficult to repeat in the bureaucratic stronghold of Vienna, but the threat of the Greens has made all three main political parties rethink their policies on such issues as nuclear energy and the environment.*

With the exception of the Greens, the other minor parties can be discounted as being of little interest. There is an extreme right-wing group numbering less than a few thousand members whose activities seem limited to putting out anti-Semitic posters and other forms of neo-Nazi propaganda.

* In the 1986 general election the Greens entered Parliament with eight seats.

There is also a Communist party with its own newspaper, the *Volkstimme* (*Voice of the People*), a journal which takes an unfailingly hostile view of all the parties' misdemeanours. But after ten years of Russian occupation after the last war, there is little to persuade even the most disgruntled Austrian worker to vote Communist. The cracks in the Communist system are particularly visible if you see them close to, as many Austrians living within a few hours of the Iron Curtain realize.

As head of state stands the president, currently the controversial Dr Kurt Waldheim. A figurehead with certain emergency powers, never so far invoked, he is theoretically above party politics though no one can deny that support from the Austrian People's Party was a major factor in Dr Waldheim's resounding victory in 1986 over his Socialist rival, Dr Kurt Steyrer. With the office of President comes a certain amount of informal power and, most important of all, the opportunity to influence the bureaucracy through certain minor appointments.

Despite the nepotism and the *Protektion* network that dominates the bureaucracy, it should not be forgotten that the 'tyranny' evoked by Viktor Adler still remains tantalizingly vulnerable to every imaginable human failing. This is likely to become more obvious as long as hundreds of jobs, which could be done at a stroke by a single computer, remain the preserve of this privileged class. But the inflexibility of the system will never tolerate the new technology. To ring directory inquiries and ask for a Vienna telephone number is a nightmare if one is in any kind of hurry. You must listen to three different answering machines which eventually pass you to an official who in turn palms you off on to the next official. Eventually, after giving the details of the subscriber's address, you hear a resounding crash as the receiver at the other end is dropped to the floor and the official walks off to return some minutes later with the relevant book. Were one not in a hurry, and were the service free, this archaic system might even seem rather quaint; as it is, every one of the fifteen minutes involved in the tortuous procedure must be paid for.

This kind of antiquated bureaucracy, resistant to reform, inevitably excludes originality and even geniality; it demands meek, pedantic minds that shrink from initiative and new ideas and are submissive to routine. If it has any virtues, beyond the fact that it is perhaps the very thing that has enabled the country to survive so many shocks over the years, it is the fallibility that gives it all a human face and which has been celebrated in countless descriptions of dealings with Austrian officialdom. One of the most poignant is that of Lord Frederic Hamilton, who as a young attaché in the 1870s at the British Embassy in Berlin worked in a building shared by the chancery of the Austro-Hungarian Embassy. The Austrian chancellor was very deaf and had entirely lost the power of regulating his voice, which was audible several hundred yards away. As Hamilton relates:

'I was at work in the chancery one day when I heard a stupendous din arising from the Austrian chancery. "The Imperial Chancellor told me," thundered this megaphone voice in stentorian tones, every word of which must have been distinctly heard in the street, "that under no circumstances whatever would Germany consent to this arrangement. If the proposal is pressed, Germany will resist it to the utmost, if necessary by force of arms. The Chancellor, in giving me this information," went on the strident voice, "impressed upon me how absolutely secret the matter must be kept. I need hardly inform your Excellency that this telegram is confidential to the highest degree."

"What is that appalling noise in the Austrian chancery?" I asked our white-headed old chancellory servant. "That is Count W dictating a cypher telegram to Vienna." This little episode has always seemed to me curiously typical of Austrian methods . . .'

And typical it remains. A young foreigner who recently made great efforts to pay his telephone bill was amazed a week later to find his telephone cut off. On ringing the authorities he eventually found that it had been an error, but that in the attempts to disconnect his line, all his neighbours had been cut off during the two previous days.

Not surprisingly, this amount of hit and miss is a good breeding-ground for scandals which eventually reach the public's notice. Cases involving naïve management and the loss of considerable amounts of money occur with monotonous regularity. In one case the entire managing board of the Voest Alpin, a steel concern founded by Hermann Goering before the war and the flagship of the country's nationalized industries, resigned in 1986 after it was discovered that millions of pounds had been lost in a foolhardy speculation in Middle East oil shares. The loss was eventually and rather drastically paid for by the forced redundancy of some 9,000 workers.

Such incompetence and dishonesty are endemic, yet the Austrian currency remains strong, locked as it is into that of West Germany. The truth of the matter is that neither the West nor the East can afford the country to destabilize, and so their investment in Austria continues apace. This promotes a prosperity which is really out of the hands of the politicians, and the day-to-day administration of government therefore has little to do with them. The disgruntled Austrian knows that there are few more futile acts than to air a grievance with an MP. This is why *Protektion* is of such importance in his dealings with the state, and it also explains the lapse in moral fibre which has so disfigured recent Austrian political history.

CHAPTER VIII

Austrian cuisine: a question of taste

'*Every Wiener Schnitzel made is a homage to Vienna and the local method of cooking. There is no compromise — even over Rindfleisch where, heaven knows, some compromise is needed to temper the dullness.*'

Edward Crankshaw, *Vienna* (1938)

It quickly becomes apparent to anyone who lingers for a few days in Austria that there is a religious quality about the relationship between the Austrian and his food. Few things are taken quite as seriously – certainly not politics or women. The passion lavished on eating and drinking is of a kind that demands dishes that appeal more to the appetite than to the senses, which results in a considerable section of the population displaying an unhappy degree of corpulence. The vast women to be seen in Vienna are particularly striking, and there are few men over fifty who do not show signs of a coronary condition brought about by over-eating. It is as if the privations of two post-war periods have instilled in the Austrian a fear that if he does not eat as much as he can he will be ill-prepared when the next period of shortage occurs.

Needless to say, *nouvelle cuisine* has completely failed to penetrate even the more fashionable restaurants. All exotic tastes are rejected – until a few years ago the kiwi fruit and the avocado were unheard of even in the most opulent delicatessens of the capital – and any dish that does not require a loosening of the belt by a few notches is considered a manifest failure.

At the time of writing the only foreign cuisines to have breached the stronghold of Austrian cooking are the Italian and the oriental. Yet, as a result of centuries of rule over very different countries, it is by no means lacking in variety. *Schokolade Palatschinken* (chocolate pancakes) from Hungary, *Knödel* (dumplings) from Czechoslavia and grilled pork from Dalmatia can all usually be found on one menu. But, like the imperial bureaucracy which once administered these lands, they have all acquired a heaviness of flavour and texture which is singularly unimaginative. Apart from in Styria, where Teuton meets Slav, there is no understanding of the complexities of salad dressing; there, however, a delicious pumpkin oil is encountered, though a few miles north of the Styrian border it is unheard of.

The principal dish in a typical Austrian dinner is invariably meat. The *Tafel Spitz* (boiled beef) and *Wiener Schnitzel* (breaded veal) are the two most popular, restaurants often competing with one another to achieve the most succulent version of the former and the largest of the latter. But even these efforts emphasize the visceral qualities of Austrian cuisine which, like the Austrian character, knows no reserve and little self-effacement.

The apotheosis of this approach can be found in the rich game dishes and the large selection of baroque puddings encountered on most menus. The most striking example of the latter must be the extraordinary *Salzburger Nockerl*, a huge fluffy mass of egg-white which takes almost an hour to prepare and which seems better suited as a prop for some debauched scene in an Erich von Stroheim film than for the dinner table. It is a disappointment to eat despite its impressive appearance, yet there must be something satisfying to the Austrian who can make short work of it all and, by demolishing such vastness, sit back with a sense of achievement.

There is also an impressive armoury of cakes, legendary in their sweetness and available in most parts of the country. Like the dumplings, many of the cakes originate from the Habsburgs' Czech possessions. Before the First World War most well-to-do families in Vienna had a Czech cook, who would produce chocolate cakes, nut cakes and, of course, the splendid *Apfelstrudel* and its relatives made with black cherries and cream.

The *Konditorei* or patisseries which supply these cakes are an essential stop in Austrian ladies' daily itineraries. Here, as well as *Strudel*, are found a number of cakes which will defeat the most ravenous Anglo-Saxon appetite. The most lethal perhaps is the rather uninspiringly named 'Marzipan Potato', though a runner-up is the extremely rich double-truffle *Torte*. The *Dobostorte*, a native of Hungary with a coating of caramel, is perhaps the finest of all these.

Between the strudels and the tortes there is a medium-weight fruit cake known as *Mehlspeis*, perhaps the healthiest of all the cakes and, as a result, a favourite with older ladies. Another popular delicacy is the *Marmor Gugelhupf*, a sponge shaped like a nineteenth-century gasometer, with a coloured exterior giving the *stucco lustro* effect implied by its name. This typically Viennese product seems to have originated in Czechoslovakia.

The most celebrated of all Viennese cakes, however, is the *Sachertorte*, named after Metternich's chef, Franz Sacher. Almost every cake establishment in the country has its own *Sachertorte* recipe, but connoisseurs recognize only two: one which is made in the Sacher Hotel and one produced by the former imperial and royal confectioners, Demel's in the Kohlmarkt in Vienna. Some years ago, after costly litigation, Demel's won the right to call its version 'original' *Sachertorte* after proving that their recipe came from a pastry cook who had worked first at the Sacher Hotel and then, after disagreement, had brought his services and his recipe intact to Demel's, with the result that Sacher had had to introduce a new recipe.

There are many who to this day denigrate Sacher's product on this ground. I for one have always found this version, without the jam filling of Demel's creation, the superior, though the latter establishment offers some compensation in the form of its Amazonian blonde waitresses dressed in sombre black silk. While the Sacher Hotel boasts some fine

Biedermeier painting to distract the eye, its somewhat truculent staff are rarely as accommodating as the *Demelinerinnen.*

Demel's is a curious place. In recent years it has become the reputed venue for clandestine meetings between the fashionable and the powerful of Vienna, and there are constant reports of its playing a role in various Freemason conspiracies. During the days of the monarchy it was a favourite haunt for women of easy virtue in search of wealthy patrons. As Virginio Gayda observed in 1916, 'Among the places of refreshment, a fashionable confectioners called Demels is famous in Vienna and this shop is the rendezvous of many ladies of the middle classes who seek and wait. Pious middle-aged ladies of the best society attend to receive and communicate the lovers' confidences.' Sometimes, in the late autumn months, the mirrored salons of Demel's still seem to breathe a curious air of *fin-de-siècle* promiscuity spiced with the whisper of intrigue.

With the exception of Sacher's, Demel's has no rivals in Vienna or indeed in the whole of Austria, though there are some who would hold that Zauner's in Bad Ischl runs Demel's a close second. In one important respect, however, Demel's is a disappointment. Its coffee is vile, and an *espresso* machine has yet to cross its parqueted threshold. Yet as Demel's is not really a coffee house this solecism is perhaps forgiveable.

The visitor to Austria may wonder why the Austrian should be fastidious about coffee when he is prepared to gorge himself indiscriminately on such a heavy and homogenous diet of meats and cakes. Paradoxically, his interest in coffee amounts almost to a scientific discipline, in which every possible combination of milk and coffee is obsessively categorized. To ask simply for 'a coffee' in an Austrian café is to elicit the blankest of expressions. Depending on the amount of milk and other ingredients desired, it will be necessary to employ various names. Thus plain black coffee is known as *'Mokka' 'Kapuziner'* has a dot of milk, and the

'*Franziskaner*' or '*Melange*' is an even lighter shade of brown. The *Melange* is something of a problem, however. In most coffee houses in Vienna it denotes half milk and half coffee, but in the Hotel Sacher and the Café Bazar in Salzburg a dash of cream is added which can leave a rather sour taste. Those who delight in masses of whipped cream should indulge in an '*Einspänner*', usually served in a glass and consisting of black coffee topped with an immoderate amount of whipped cream. On the other hand, great care should be taken to avoid ordering the '*Kaiser Melange*', which was inspired by the spartan taste of the Emperor Franz Josef and consists of black coffee and two egg yolks. Few things taste more vile.

Devotion to coffee is most developed in Vienna and eastern Austria, where the coffee house is an unassailable institution thriving on a laziness and lethargy which demands caffeine and some degree of cosy comfort at regular intervals. The origins of the very first coffee house can be traced to 1683 when Vienna was besieged by the Turks. Months before Sobieski's cavalry drove the Infidel from the gates of the city a certain Herr Kolschitzky, a coffee merchant by profession, was helping the Austrians to achieve victory in a more subtle way. Disguised as a pasha he traded among the Turkish camps, taking detailed notes of their positions and numbers. When the siege was raised the Habsburgs did not forget their brave spy. For the first time in the history of the Holy Roman Empire, a licence was granted to establish a coffee house – Kolschitzky's 'Kaffee Schrank'. This remarkable institution was such a success that coffee houses became an essential feature of central European life, playing an indispensable role in business, politics and social affairs as well as providing a venue for darker forms of intrigue.

Perhaps the most celebrated example of coffee-house machination took place in the Café Central one cold winter in 1913. Here a certain Herr Bronstein would regularly order coffee and play chess. A harmless activity, it seemed to the ever-vigilant Vienna secret police, who were not to know that 'Bronstein' and his chess partner, later to become better known as Trotsky and Stalin, were planning moves that would affect more than a few chess pieces. It is one of the typically Austrian ironies of the Great War that when the news was brought of the revolution in St Petersburg a nonplussed official jokingly remarked, 'I suppose someone will now tell me that Herr Bronstein thought this up in the Café Central.'

The Central has recently been restored, and its spies and revolutionaries replaced by an army of civil servants who work in the nearby ministries. Like most Viennese businessmen, they seem to prefer discussing their affairs in leisurely fashion in a coffee house rather than in an office. This attachment to cafés for business as well as pleasure will ensure that the institution does not die, even though the number of cafés in the city has declined to only 400 compared with 4,000 just before the war. The Vienna city council, mindful of their historical and architectural interest and perhaps also of their appeal to tourists in search of the atmosphere of *The Third Man* and Johann Strauss, has begun to preserve and restore some of those that remain, though often, alas, with disastrous results. The Café Sperl, for example, on the Gumpendorferstrasse in Vienna's Sixth District, demonstrated in its restoration recently that the essential qualities of the coffee house elude the city's *soi-disante* 'conservation experts'. In the first place, it is impossible to 'renovate' an old coffee house, and any attempt to restore its fabric should be mild rather than drastic. The faded parquet and furnishings and the smoke-stained walls are as much a part of its charm as the light fittings and *Jugendstil* tables. Secondly, if restoration is to go ahead, the last people who should be involved are the *Denkmalamt* or monuments authority, who, suffering from all the weaknesses inherent in Austrian bureaucracy, are remarkably lacking in either sensitivity or taste. At the Café Sperl this was amply demonstrated by the no doubt historically correct notion that as the café dates from the late 1880s all the superb 1905 panelling was 'inaccurate' and therefore had to be ripped out. It was replaced with a paper-masquerading-as-wood substance which, though fashionable in the 1880s, is so unappealing that regulars no longer feel comfortable in the place. Another *folie scientifique* was the introduction of bright lights which destroy the shadowy corners that were once Sperl's great joy. Some might argue that this is a small price to pay for the great improvement in sanitation that has taken place – it is true that one no longer runs the risk of sharing a table with a cockroach – but there are many more who will not go anywhere near the place these days because of its unhappy transformation.

Not so far away from the Café Sperl, the celebrated Kaiserbrundl Café, with its exotic red plush alcoves and niches, classical columns and mirrors, all resounding to the music of Verdi, has suffered an even crueller fate. This unique and theatrical interior was allowed by the 'guardians' of Vienna's architectural heritage to be turned first into a brothel – for which purpose, it must be conceded, its décor was singularly apt – and then into a discothèque which, not illogically, found the presence of such classical elements ill-suited to the rhythms of modern rock and so promptly removed them.

Notwithstanding the *Denkmalamt*'s efforts, several characteristic cafés have survived. Of these the most legendary is Hawelka's which, except in the early mornings when there is very much the hush of the morning after an excessive night, is always bustling with activity. Herr Hawelka, one of the few Austrians left who know how to tie their own bow ties, is of the old school and unfailingly courteous. His waiters, Engelbert and Eduard, combine that harassed manner tinged with a hint of cynical rapacity which is the true hallmark of the Vienna coffee-house waiter.

Of the other cafés in Vienna the Bräunerhof also has some characteristic waiters who, in their smiling, disregarding nonchalance, are capable of reducing a normally unflappable Scottish laird to a fit of uncontrollable pique. For those in search of something more subdued, however, the Café Prückel is probably the most curious survival. Once the most ornate and opulent of cafés – its lavishness gave rise to the epithet 'Prückel Baroque' – it is now rather austere. Its high, bleak ceilings still bear the paint which was hurriedly applied in the 1950s after the Russian cavalry, which had used it to stable their horses, moved out. The 1950s furniture, grey but comfortable, and the wilting plants contribute powerfully to the impression of *'Osteuropa'* decay. The clientèle are eccentric, as are the staff, who include one remarkable waiter who is as witty a remnant of the old school as any to be found in Austria and who insists on cracking a joke every time he presents a bill.

While the traditional coffee house with all its idiosyncrasies is preserved in Vienna, it is on the decline in other Austrian cities. In Graz all the great old cafés were converted into shoe shops or banks ten years ago. The Nordstern above the Hauptplatz has survived, but its rooms now resound to the whirr and bleep of electronic games. In Innsbruck the energetic Tyrolean has no time to lounge around in coffee houses, while in Carinthia the urban culture has never reached the degree of sophistication of neighbouring Styria. Only in Salzburg has something of the old world been preserved in two marvellous coffee houses. The Café Bazar, next to the overrated Österreicher Hof hotel, still recalls the heady days of the 1930s when it was the haunt of the English *beau monde* on vacation. With its elegant panelled rooms, its unrivalled strudel and its charming waitresses, it remains one of the great coffee houses of Europe, though during the Salzburg Festival it is Americans rather than Britons who occupy its sofas. Café Tomaselli across the river is also not without charm, though for some reason it has never been particularly popular among visitors. That great pre-War traveller Robert Byron may be partly responsible for this. In *Europe Through the Looking Glass* (1926), he makes fun of its founder, Herr Tomaselli.

After negotiating the pitfalls and complexities of the world of the Austrian coffee house, the visitor will find himself treading on something of a gastronomic minefield when he uncorks his first bottle of Austrian wine, especially if he has in mind the events of the summer of 1985 when the discovery of the antifreeze agent diethylene glycol in bottles of Austrian white wine led overnight to the collapse of the country's wine exports, the bankruptcy of many growers and the arrest of even more dealers. More than fifteen million litres of contaminated wine were seized, and what was dubbed 'the great Austrian wine scandal' was broken down into no fewer than six separate scandals involving wine and fruit juices. These, to summarize briefly, were:

1. the illegal sale of *Qualität* certificates for wines that did not meet statutory requirements for such labels;
2. the adding of diethylene glycol to sweeten Burgenland wines so that their sugar content qualified them for *Auslese* labels commanding higher prices;
3. the discovery in supermarkets of 'artificial wine' made of water, chemicals and the 'refuse of grapes';
4. the discovery that three companies were adding diethylene glycol to grape juices;
5. the watering down of table wines by as much as thirty per cent;
6. most distressing of all, the discovery that every second glass of Austrian red wine had never seen a single red grape and was in fact white wine coloured by the addition of cheap Italian red or red grape refuse.

This formidable amount of doctoring was not, it is significant to note, the work of a single mastermind raking in vast sums of money. Rather, it was the work of hundreds of corrupt individuals who felt there was nothing dangerous in doctoring wines. Certainly it is clear that few believed they were guilty of doing anything immoral.

The ultimate irony in this extraordinary affair is that had it not been for the greed of one dealer who attempted to offset a suspiciously large amount of antifreeze against tax it is unlikely that any of these scandals would have come to light. Once the scandal was revealed – in West Germany, it may be noted, not in Austria – the authorities and the bureaucracy set about rounding up the offenders with uncharacteristic energy. With consummate skill a law was devised which is so bureaucratic that to this day it remains largely unworkable among the country's 53,000 wine growers. The visitor to Austria is unlikely to be aware of the complications of the 'strictest wine law in Europe', as it has been hailed by the Austrian authorities. Its twenty-five-point code has been enforced with varying degrees of enthusiasm. Some bottle labels remain unchanged while others need a technical dictionary to comprehend.

Nowadays there is no reason to be worried about drinking Austrian wines, though many of them should be avoided on account of their acidity and thinness. On the whole Austrian wine is drunk rather young. The financial dependence of the growers on quick sales and a high turnover discourages many growers from allowing their wines to age more than two or three years. In addition to this, the bleak climate, with its harsh winters and short summers, does not encourage sound vintage wines.

Red wines often seem at first glance to be a disappointment. In their paleness of colour and anaemic body they seem to resemble jam juice but without any pungent fruitiness. In Burgenland the Blaufränkisch, made from a grape originally from Charlemagne's Franconia, is tolerable. Another worthy red is the *Zweigelt* crossbreed grown in the picturesque Wachau valley of the Danube. Understandably, as these cannot compare with the reds to the south and east of Austria, it is the whites that remain most popular.

Of these the *Gruner Veltliner*, which accounts for thirty per cent of all wines sold in the country, is pleasant if at times thin, and it is unique to Austria. It has a faintly peppery aftertaste which makes it an agreeable companion to dumplings and *Wiener Schnitzel*. Also to be found along the banks of the Danube west of Vienna is the most impressive of the Austrian whites, the Rhine *Riesling*. These vines grow in particular abundance around the ruins of the once formidable fortress of Durnstein which commands the dramatic valley of the Danube between Melk and Krems.

A little way south of Graz, the Styrian capital only a few miles from the Yugoslav frontier, the foothills of the Julian Alps are endowed with a grape found in no other part of the world from which the *Schilcher Rosé* is made. This wine has been a Styrian delicacy since medieval times and, though something of an acquired taste, it is in summer one of the more refreshing wines to be found in Austria.

Another refreshing drink which makes its appearance in the autumn is *Sturm*, made partly from grape juice and partly from wine. In view of its strength and the effect it is known to have on those who are disarmed by its yeasty fizz, its name is surprisingly apt. *Sturm*, along with the best of the young Austrian white wines, is usually to be found in one of the *Heurigen* or taverns which fill the valleys of the Vienna woods above the Austrian capital. These celebrated institutions, as much a part of Vienna as the coffee house, have suffered from tourism in recent decades. In Grinzing there is hardly a single *Heurigen* left which does not reel from the combined onslaught of Italian and German busloads deposited here in search of a 'genuine Austrian evening'. In the more remote districts the situation is a little better, and in Sievering there is one *Heurigen*, open only eight weeks of the year, alas, which preserves a sleepy calm that is virtually extinct. Unless visited in these circumstances the *Heurigen* is unlikely to appeal. Crowded, noisy and expensive with often astringent wine, it is the exact antithesis of that romantic setting familiar to followers of Erich von Stroheim or Richard Tauber.

In some years Austrian wine is undrinkable, though it has not been necessary since the fourteenth century to pour the entire vintage into the foundations of the cathedral tower. For an alternative, those who take their beer seriously will derive some satisfaction from the fine, light Austrian lagers which are the traditional accompaniment to soup, though they do not stand comparison with the ales of nearby Moravia and Bohemia. Or there is the home-made *Schnapps* which every Austrian farmer proudly produces for his guest. Either as an aperitif or as a digestif, during sharp winter months in the mountains this is unrivalled.

With so many tempting drinks available at a fraction of what such beverages cost in more northern countries it is not surprising that a large number of Austrians regularly get drunk.* The climate, with its hot, listless summers, along with the Austrian tendency towards melancholy, is probably to blame. In any event, those visitors who acquire a taste for these drinks in the absence of licensing laws may find developing an Austrian figure easier than they thought.

*Fourteen per cent of the population are alcohol-dependent, according to the Salzburg daily, *Nachrichten*.

CHAPTER IX

Vienna and Danube Austria

'On approaching Vienna faith and idealism vanish. It is this moral void that makes most foreigners and many Austrians feel perennially strangers in the Austrian capital.'

Wickham Steed, *The Habsburg Monarchy* (1914)

In spite of all the negative characteristics of the Viennese themselves, Vienna still manages to retain a universal reputation, dating perhaps from the days of Johann Strauss or the Congress of Vienna, for 'gaiety'. But of this reputed gaiety the stranger sees little. What he does see is a whole population occasionally interrupting its moods of misanthropy and xenophobia with attempts at being gay. Everywhere there hangs an air of lethargy and cynicism, from which all the signs of a living present – energy, ambition, faith, idealism – seem remote. There is little spontaneous merriment, and the burden of centuries of absolutist rule seems to weigh down from the high grey façades which in the winter months conspire to exclude even a glimpse of the sky. Like a soporific drug cushioning the Viennese from the present, the past is inhaled in every corner of the city, from the Prater in the east, with its remarkable giant Ferris wheel, to the inns of Sievering in the west.

The people of Vienna are completely different from western and Alpine Austrians, with a different set of morals and attitudes from the rest of the country. They regard their city as incomparable – as indeed it is, after a fashion. No European capital has such a stately, imperial air – despite decades of Socialist rule, the double-headed eagle still broods overhead wherever you go – and no other European capital has such delightful surroundings. On a Sunday afternoon, wandering among the deserted cobbled streets around the Minorites Church, one can almost hear Castlereagh's footsteps marking the way from the Palais Dietrichstein, where he was lodged, to the Ballhausplatz during the Congress of Vienna. Close by, the chancery gates still seem firmly closed to the 1848 mob eager for Metternich's blood, while across the grass the vast megalomaniac pile of the New Hofburg, with its balcony overlooking the Heldenplatz, inevitably conjures up that day in 1938 when Austrians stood roaring with delight at the only man ever to have addressed them from this vantage-point – Adolf Hitler. Through the Hofburg, in the Michaelerplatz, Adolf Loos flaunts his concept of streamlined architecture, free from 'the crime of ornament', in his bleak, classical Goldman and Salatch House. Through an arch on the right, the Palais Pallavicini still seems to resound to Orson Welles's footsteps and the Harry Lime theme.

In all these places time seems to have stood still. Elsewhere, however, in the Café Zartl in the Rasumofskystrasse on a late winter's evening, or in the Gmoa Keller on the Heumarkt, smoky, shabby and run by two ancient Hungarian ladies whose wit, manners and charm, like their rooms, have remained unchanged for decades, one encounters a different Vienna. Beneath the appearance of gaiety among the habitués there is evidence of much hard work; beneath the superficial politeness there is much real courtesy; alongside the childishness, a great shrewdness and knowledge of mankind; and amid scepticism and carelessness, a fabulous wealth of talent.

The level of talent in Vienna is remarkably high, though it is often without object or intelligible purpose. In the words of the great Austrian writer Hermann Bahr, it is like an abandoned piano, containing all potentialities of sound, but silent. In the Gmoa Keller one might hear a brilliant tenor sing Noel Coward, or a gifted painter discourse on art, but until they leave Vienna there will be no challenge to fashion this raw talent into something more durable than the sporadic efforts of the dilettante. The 'stupidity' and 'crassness' of the Viennese and of the Austrians generally, by which strangers are so often struck, arises not from lack of wits but from the absence of any opportunity for the application of intelligence. The beginning of positive intelligence is the discipline of attention, and few Viennese have ever been schooled to concentrate their minds on matters more important than parties or concerts, their relations or domestic trivia.

The absolutism which is largely responsible for this melancholy situation is expressed first by the sprawling and rather ugly Hofburg, and then by the uninspired but prettily situated Schönbrunn, summer palace of the Habsburgs. Although they are outshone by the maverick genius of Lukas von Hildebrandt's Belvedere Palace, built not for a Habsburg but for Prince Eugène of Savoy, both are better known and more frequently visited.

Schönbrunn, originally planned in 1695 by Fischer von Erlach to rival Versailles, was left incomplete by that great master. The costly campaigns of the War of the Spanish Succession prevented him from realizing his dreams, and what was to be his *magnum opus* became the unfortunate vehicle for Nicholas Pacassi's mediocre talents a generation later. None the less, its garden, with its high clipped hedges and fake Roman ruins, combines grandeur with a characteristically Viennese intimacy which is wholly absent in Versailles.

The hill on which Fischer planned to extend his masterpiece is now crowned by a pleasing Doric loggia, the Gloriette, the first building ever erected in Austria to commemorate a military victory – that of Kolin in 1757 in the Seven Years War. Here the Viennese obsession with the past is impressively vindicated, for while almost every other city in Europe has been forced to endure a proliferation of crude modern tower blocks, Vienna presents a virtually unspoilt panorama which would be instantly recognizable to Napoleon, who gazed out from these arches when he made Schönbrunn his headquarters after the Battle of Wagram in 1809. The vast scale of the great Gothic Cathedral of St

Stephen's still rises unchallenged by any other building in the city. To the west, in the hills of the Vienna woods, the most modern sight seems to be Otto Wagner's marble and copper-domed Steinhof church, a mysterious building situated high above a lunatic asylum where inmates mutter and stare while they walk in the pine woods, in grotesque contrast, so charateristically Viennese, to this cold and geometrically precise church.

To the east the only obvious eyesore, all the more horrible in its unspoilt setting, is the ugly mass of the Vienna hospital, two slabs of brown which in scale, colour and design represent all that is most insensitive in modern Viennese architecture.

In the park between the Gloriette and the *Schloss* there is a curious frippery of a building containing the original '*schöner Brunnen*' ('beautiful spring') which, in accordance with the canons of Vitruvius and Palladio, made this such a suitable place to erect a summer residence. During the summer a devoted old lady offers for a few schillings a glass of this crystal-clear water which, like all the city's water – the best of any European capital – comes through a series of viaducts from the Schneeberg, the highest mountain in Lower Austria some twenty-five miles south. In another part of the park is a zoo, where a number of interesting nineteenth-century buildings are still used – often to the outrage of animal lovers – to house the more exotic specimens.

The interior of Schönbrunn is a disappointment. The most interesting rooms and those which command the best views seem to have been appropriated, as in most of the Habsburgs' former palaces, as grace-and-favour apartments for privileged civil servants. Instead, the visitor who joins one of the large guided tours, which is the only way of entering the public interior of the building, is led through a curiously barren series of rooms where most of the furniture is surprisingly mediocre and, with the exception of the memorial room of the ill-fated Duke of Reichstadt, Napoleon's son, entirely lacking in historical interest.

Beyond the western gates of Schönbrunn lies Hietzing, a picturesque suburb full of villas and low three-storey houses set in gardens. In the Auhofstrasse, in a secluded corner not far from the main road, stands the Café Dommayer, an old haunt of Johann Strauss and a most agreeable place to spend an hour or two. Its waiters are a little brusque, but few coffee-houses in Vienna offer such a peaceful garden in which to enjoy the warm summer evenings.

Back in the town centre it is the Hofburg which gives the most satisfying picture of what life was like for the ruling dynasty during the *Franzjosefzeit*. Again, as is so often the case in Austria, the only way of seeing the imperial apartments is by guided tour, though there is little to be said of them except to point out a dramatic example of the lengths a woman will go to preserve her figure in the room containing the Empress Elizabeth's gymnastic equipment.

Other parts of the Hofburg are given over to state entertainment rooms, the Spanish Riding School – that most polished centre of *haute école* – and the National Library. With the possible exception of the Banquet Hall in Schloss Frain in Vranov, Moravia, the library, with its huge oval dome crowning a veritable cathedral dedicated to learning, is arguably the most spectacular of Fischer von Erlach's secular creations. It is certainly the most satisfying secular building the Habsburgs left in their capital, and the subsequent additions to the palace seem like irrelevancies scattered by lesser craftsmen at the foot of Fischer's genius. Even the Leopoldinische Trakt, Leopold's apartments, sumptuously decorated under Maria Theresa, seems uninspired and lightweight in comparison.

So overpowering and pervasive is the Baroque language in Vienna that one searches almost in vain for the release a cool Gothic interior might afford. The vast Gothic cathedral is always too crowded to be able to enjoy the calm normally associated with this style, and it is only in the remarkable church known as Maria am Gestade, behind Fischer's bombed and unhappily restored Bohemian Chancery on the

Judenplatz, that there is a chance to escape the exuberant Baroque chaos.

In the Middle Ages this church stood on a tributary arm of the Danube which was subsequently diverted. The church was started in the twelfth century and the choir which is attached to it with a pleasing asymmetry dates from 1330 to 1353. The dark, solemn interior of this humble edifice, in which the fastidious craftsmanship of the Gothic age is refreshingly understated, envelops the visitor in a world completely removed from the pomp and special effects which mark so many churches in the city. The church of Maria am Gestade is not popular with the Viennese, and its tall, elegant filigree tower which once watched over fishermen is now the shrine of the city's Czech population who, numbering only a few devout souls, leave this uncharacteristic Viennese building always seeming deserted and calm.

Understatement in any form of life or the arts is rarely to be encountered in Vienna, but after the Baroque period there developed a style which allowed for a certain amount of understatement and with it an approachability which was to be a refreshing change from all that happened before and much that was to occur afterwards. It was part of that extraordinary cultural phenomenon referred to as Biedermeier, the aesthetic expression of the Metternich era which for all its oppression of the liberal spirit could not impede the prosperity of the middle class. It resulted in that class sacrificing an active role in politics and devoting itself to homely pursuits. Comfort and above all respectability were the order of the day, though there was much lightness and gentleness beneath it.

In Vienna, apart from in Hietzing where the Biedermeier villas are under attack by the sprouting of new apartment blocks, the best survival of this era is to be seen in the Josefstadt or Eighth District, where the winding Lenaugasse and Langegasse still preserve many fine classical Biedermeier houses. To wander along these streets is to enjoy a part of the city in which the sky is not obscured by vast nineteenth-century buildings. In the Lenaugasse every house opens onto a courtyard of striking beauty or interest. Behind one of them rises the classical symmetry of a college for boys erected in the late eighteenth century, all yellow stucco and delicate pilasters. Behind another door there is a courtyard of almost Dalmatian character with a high gable, potted plants and thick grey masonry.

The nearby Langegasse contains several gardens behind its rather austere façades, affording an amount of green few other parts of the city enjoy. Beyond the Doric portico of one house there stretches a lawn of almost English lushness, while the old bakery in the same street has a courtyard and a gate leading onto a garden in the manner of a seventeenth-century Cambridge college.

In the middle of all this understatement only the great church of the Piarists, Maria Treu, designed probably by Hildebrandt, strikes a different, heavier note. But here, the square on the Piaristengasse in front of it allows the building a space the Baroque creations of the First District do not enjoy, and the entire ensemble is one of Vienna's most pictur-esque *coups d'œil*.

At the end of the Piaristengasse, the Lerchenfelderstrasse contains, at no. 13, a remarkable series of narrow courtyards, rather sinister in the winter. The Adlerhof in the nearby Siebensterngasse or 'Road of the Seven Stars' is an even more striking example of this barrack-like architecture, while between the Mariahilferstrasse and the Gumperdor-ferstrasse, the most spectacular of all these unique relics of early nineteenth-century high-density housing seems set either for demolition or drastic restoration at the hands of the *Denkmalamt*.

Such Biedermeier buildings make up one of the most important architectural ensembles left in Europe, but because they receive little attention from tourists or the Viennese these precious jewels lie neglected and often broken up. Only the public buildings of the era, like the exquisite theatre in the Josefstadt, survive and enjoy some guarantee of immunity.

But this vandalism is likely to pass all but the most thorough visitor by. With only a few days to spare in the capital his attention will be held first by the Baroque and then by the inescapable blight of the later nineteenth century, exemplified in the megalomania of the Ringstrasse.

It would be interesting though doubtless futile to speculate to what extent the enormous amount of high nineteenth-century building has exerted an unhappy influence on the Viennese. When the city walls were demolished in 1857, virtually overnight the wonderful promenades which afforded fine views of the surrounding countryside disappeared, and up went the vast ten-storey palaces of the new Ringstrasse. The architecture dominates the pedestrian – he cannot view it on any terms of equality, but must weave his way overshadowed by heavy cornices at every turn. In place of the city walls several fine gardens were planted, but these, though welcome in a city with little green, cannot compensate for the loss of space.

In the small but highly interesting museum of the city of Vienna, on the Karlsplatz near Fischer's magnificent Karlskirche, there are several models of the city, painstakingly made of matchboxes, which show the capital before and after the razing of the walls. As this museum also contains a number of rooms of the Biedermeier and rococo eras, it offers the visitor a useful insight into the city's interiors before the extravagant tastelessness of the late nineteenth century descended. It also contains the reaction against this excess which caused that remarkable flowering of ingenious architecture known as *Jugendstil* or art nouveau. In a corner in the uppermost storey is Adolf Loos's sitting room, unmistakable in its Anglo-Saxon inspiration and solid craftsmanship, which he bequeathed to the city that so rarely tolerated his buildings or ideas.

Those who visit Vienna for its museums will of course find much to occupy many grey afternoons. The Kunsthistorisches Museum, with its collections of Breughel and Velasquez and its Italian Renaissance works, is one of the great art galleries of the world. Those who spend a few hours here should also not neglect the old Habsburg treasury, which is now housed in the Hofburg. The celebrated Cellini salt-cellar, the great sword of Charlemagne and the Habsburg crown jewels are the most spectacular of the exhibits displayed here.

Though the Belvedere palace, which houses a number of fine paintings by Klimt, Schiele, Kokoschka and that most deranged soul of them all in *fin-de-siècle* Vienna, Richard Gerstl, can be seen as the most 'Viennese' of the museums, by far the most memorable and expressive of what Stefan Zweig called 'the world of yesterday' is the curious and rarely visited museum of military history contained in the brick arsenal beyond. More than any other institution of the old empire, the army was all-pervasive. Every Austrian man, unless medically exempted, had to do military service – even the artists whose canvases fill the Belvedere. Egon Schiele served in Bohemia, Adolf Loos in lower Austria, where his insistence on designing his own uniform with American pockets infuriated the High Command, and Oskar Kokoschka was a dragoon subaltern on the Russian front.

Through the rather Ruskinian 'Objekt I' of the arsenal complex, the 'moorish'-style museum designed by Hansens as a tribute to the Habsburgs' armies and as a symbol of their unity in strength (*viribus unitis*) is an undeniably bizarre sight. Inside, the rooms are rich in the colourful uniforms which characterized the art of war in the eighteenth and nineteenth centuries. But it is downstairs, beyond the cabinets of the Mannlicher rifles, which offers the most memorable part of the collection. Here, at the end of a corridor, lies a sombre room with black curtains. In one corner stands a strangely familiar Austro-Daimler of about 1911. In another part of the room is a portrait of the Archduke Franz Ferdinand, whose assassination at Sarajevo in 1914 provoked the Armageddon of the First World War. Between photographs of the archduke's final car journey, outstretched in a glass cabinet, lies his blood-stained uniform, its buttons still shining between the cuts in the tunic where the surgeon's knife desperately tried to save the heir to the Habsburg throne. It is a gruesome sight, devastating in its capacity to arouse a frisson of that fateful St Vitus's day, and no other memorial in Europe encapsulates the end of the old order so concisely and powerfully.

Retracing one's steps past the Belvedere back to the centre of Vienna, a taste for the macabre can be further indulged in the vaults of the Capuchin church on the Neuemarkt, though in contrast to the Archduke's room in the Military Museum this subterranean mausoleum of the Habsburgs has little atmosphere. Despite the solemn demands inscribed on the walls for SILENTIUM, there is that unforgettable cacophony of the guide attempting to speak English in one corner and the school group demanding explanation in German in another; it is one of the drawbacks of visiting museums in Vienna that the imposition of a guide is more often than not *de rigueur*.

To escape the weighty presence of the Habsburg past, the Prater, opened to the public by that harbinger of the Enlightenment, Joseph II, is perhaps the easiest solution. Through the squalor of the Landstrasse, down the Rasumofskystrasse, passing that noble family's neo-classical palace and beyond the Café Zartl, one must walk a good half hour to reach the tributary of the Danube which since Otto Wagner's 'regulation' at the beginning of the century is all that remains of the great river in the heart of Vienna. On the other side the Leopoldstadt awaits, with the chestnut avenues of the former imperial park and the monument which, thanks to the film *The Third Man*, has come to symbolize Vienna – the Prater Wheel. On an autumn afternoon, when the colours of the park below are just turning, there is an inspiring ride to be taken in this marvel of nineteenth-century technology, with its superlative views to the east towards Bratislava and the great Hungarian Plain.

Between here and the Hungarian frontier lies a strip of land, a few hundred square miles in area, which was awarded to Austria by the Treaty of St Germain in 1919. The province of Burgenland, the market garden of Austria, is the

Danubian Austrians' native rural environment as much as the city of Vienna is his urban home. Partly because many of its inhabitants are of Hungarian and Croatian peasant stock, it has a backwardness and a sleepy calm usually associated with eastern Europe, and it has yet to suffer the tourist invasion that has already engulfed the western provinces of Salzburg and Tyrol

Eisenstadt, the capital of the province, has however suffered some damage from urban redevelopment, though in the park surrounding the Esterházys' extravagant eighteenth-century palace the eastern sleepiness reasserts itself. The *Schloss* is inseparably linked with the name of Joseph Haydn, who came to the town in 1761 to take over the direction of Prince Esterházy's orchestra, and it is possible to imagine that the curiously melancholy landscape sometimes finds expression in the works he composed here.

The mood of the landscape is at its most haunting not far from Eisenstadt in the small wine town of Rust, on the Neusiedler See. Since medieval times Rust has been famous for its wine. More recently it has become renowned among nature lovers for the frequency with which storks visit and build their nests on the town's countless medieval chimneys. From the top of the church tower there is a spectacular view over the town to the Leitha hills and the vast expanse of water which is the closest the Austrians have to a sea of their own.

Unfortunately, the number of old guest houses has declined since the beginning of the 1980s and a new and spectacularly out-of-keeping hotel seems to be the only place to spend the night. The views from the rooms overlooking the edge of the lake partly compensate – but only partly – for the ugliness of the entire structure which, built in the 'Alpine Revival' style, is as out of place here as a wooden chalet would be in Naples.

Off the beaten track, which in Burgenland means away from the main roads to Budapest and Sopron, the villages have retained some of their simplicity and an almost Mediterranean approach to life. At Steinbruck, near the Austrian army's exercise grounds, the main inn consists of one long barn of a space filled with trinkets and souvenirs including one velvet banner proclaiming the eccentric message 'Greetings from Libya'. The local village men come here to play cards. The girls, dressed to the nines on a Saturday evening, giggle and sip wine under the ever-vigilant eye of the patron. The entire atmosphere is more what one would expect to find in the Veneto than this far north of the Alps. The jollity is neither forced nor excessive, and there is a philosophical, rather relaxed attitude to good wine and food which is so often missing in the noisy, hearty inns of Alpine Austria.

Of the many castles (*Burgen*) to be found in the province, two demand a visit. Schloss Hof, built for Prince Eugène of Savoy, was immortalized by Canaletto in two famous views. The gardens have long gone to ruin but the palace has been painstakingly restored, its frescos and plasterwork escaping the usual heavy hand of the modern Austrian craftsman. Set low, the entire structure still dominates the surrounding countryside in seigneurial splendour.

In the summer the more strongly fortified Schloss Lockenhausen combines dramatic architecture with a far too little known music festival which is one of the most enjoyable in Europe. The Baroque church below the castle in the village square is the venue for chamber concerts whose standards often equal those of more fashionable Salzburg. The castle itself has the unexpected but welcome merit of also being a hotel with comfortably furnished rooms, all too cold in the winter, alas, when the castle is closed, but ideal in the summer for those unable to face the tortuous journey back to Vienna or Eisenstadt.

To the south of the province the land becomes undulating. The sunsets still have an eastern hue to them, and there are few more remote places to be than in one of the half-ruined châteaux which seem to be dotted around Güssing and which, with their moats silted up, their parks overgrown and their owners long absent or senile, represent the last remnants of a now-forgotten order.

For some reason, partly perhaps to do with this eastern calm, the inhabitants of Burgenland, who are short and sturdy like the Hungarians under whose rule the province remained backward for centuries, have a reputation for being somewhat slow-witted. Burgenland jokes abound in Vienna, and they reached a peak during the chancellorship of Dr Fred Sinowatz from 1983 to 1986. Dr Sinowatz, whose simple lifestyle and unforgettable features are redolent of the gypsy-Magyar strain in some of the inhabitants of this part of Austria, was considered by Austrians living west of Vienna as an abomination. 'The Burgenland Stalinist', the Salzburg papers dubbed him. 'The Gypsy Chancellor' was the verdict of others. It would be difficult to overestimate the role this crass contempt many Austrians felt for Dr Sinowatz's origins played in his political downfall. As a Burgenländer, it was widely assumed that he could not govern; he simply 'did not look right' as Austrian chancellor. Yet, as is so often the case when fun is made at the expense of a minority, the Burgen-länders do not seem any less intelligent than their fellow Austrians in the Alpine provinces, and in appearance at least they do not fall victim to Belloc's jibe:

> Here we have the Alpine race,
> O what a broad and foolish face.

But when all is said and done the attractions of Burgenland are unlikely to detain us for long, and our view of Danube Austria is more likely to be derived from our time spent in Vienna rather than Eisenstadt.

Travelling west or even south towards Graz one encoun-ters almost immediately those inescapable features of Alpine countryside so absent in Burgenland – the peaks of the east-ern Alps. A different mentality exists here, fashioned not by the dry and windy climate of the Eastern Marches but, dur-ing the summer, by the almost daily minor apocalypse which is an Alpine thunderstorm, and in winter by that mixture of magic and chaos which dresses these lands in snow for months on end.

As soon as one is on the Semmering, and the flat mass of Vienna drops into the fog behind, a sensation not unlike relief is felt. The scenery of Alpine Austria is spectacular, the mentality of the Alpine Austrian less so but both are a refreshing change from Vienna, and must be seen now in their true context, divorced from the strange part of Eastern Europe we have just briefly toured.

CHAPTER X

Alpine Austria

'You can easily vulgarise the seaside but you can never civilise a mountain.'
G. E. R. Gedye, *A Wayfarer in Austria* (1928)

However influential climate and scenery might be in making the Austrian of the Alps so different from his kinsman of the Danube, there is undeniably a factor of race to be considered. The Austrians of Tyrol and Vorarlberg have that mixture of Celt and Teuton in them which is associated with the German Swiss, while those of the province of Salzburg are very similar to the Bavarians of southern Germany. In the beautiful land of East Tyrol the Celtic strain is particularly prevalent. Only in Styria and Carinthia does the Slav influence mingle with the German, and there it is the dreamy but none the less energetic south Slav, not the melancholy Czech, whose temperament mixes with these southernmost Germans in Europe.

The presence of so many Slovenes in Carinthia produces a rather combustible, xenophobic Austrian who attempts to deny the presence of any Slav blood in his veins by acting in an almost paranoid pan-German fashion. Like a religious convert, this Austrian parades his German attributes more proudly than the Austrian with solely German antecedents. For centuries under the Habsburgs to be Slav meant in many ways to be a second-class citizen, though many Slavs reached positions of great responsibility in the empire. During the Third Reich this division of races was taken several grotesque steps further when the Slavs were relegated to the position of *'Untermenschen'* (sub-humans), a label which is still applied to them by those Austrians who are insecure about their own racial origin.

Racial differences aside, the Austrians of Styria and Carinthia are in many ways similar to those of Tyrol, Salzburg and Vorarlberg, linked as they are by the dramatic background of the Alps. In an environment where nature's capacity for destruction, in the form of avalanches, earthquakes and snowstorms, is as evident now as it was centuries ago before the advent of modern science and medicine, the popularity of the Catholic Church is not surprising, and superstition is rife in the Alpine villages. In one small village called Rinn, for example, the inhabitants continue to cling tenaciously to the legend of a young child who was murdered there by the Jews in medieval times. Despite protests from the Vatican and the local bishop, worried about potential anti-Semitic overtones, the villagers continue to worship in the church dedicated to 'Anderl' of Rinn, the child who was so cruelly despatched. Each year a procession commemorating his death at the hands of the Jews takes place, involving nearly all the villagers.

Other less controversial shrines, votive chapels and roadside crucifixes are scattered throughout the length and breadth of the countryside. Some, like the great shrine of Mariazell, have become national monuments. Others, though less celebrated, continue to extract dozens of votive offerings every month from devout pilgrims.

Not surprisingly this part of Austria is traditionally a stronghold of the 'Blacks', the clerical People's Party which, though less closely associated with the church than at earlier times in its history, none the less commands among its supporters the majority of practising Austrian Catholics. Only in Carinthia, where the Slovene question is for some, deliberately or subconsciously, a priority, does the People's Party concede its majority to other parties.

Perhaps because the Alpine views are so dramatic, and the combination of clouds, castles, sky and mountains so impressive, there is a feeling of human inadequacy which instills a certain humility rarely encountered in the city of Vienna. Whoever has seen the stormclouds gather round the pass between Salzburg and Styria at Schloss Werfen or some other picturesque defile can hardly fail to be aware of the ability the landscape possesses to make one blindingly aware of man's insignificance. Nowhere perhaps is this more apparent than in the Tyrol where, south of Innsbruck, the great Brenner Pass and the mountains of Berg Isel form a sublime scenery against which the Tyrolean capital seems just an elegant toy.

Though the city is dwarfed by the sheer peaks which rise around it, there is much nobility in its architecture. The Hofkirche, one of the greatest Renaissance monuments in Europe, owes its existence to Emperor Maximilian I's choice of Innsbruck rather than Vienna as his capital from 1493 to 1519. Inside the Hofkirche we move amidst a noble company of kings and emperors – twenty-eight lifesize figures, actual or imaginary ancestors of Maximilian, who guard his tomb. They are the work of various artists, as the casting of the bronze went on from 1511 until 1548. They vary greatly in artistic merit, but the majority show a fabulous wealth of late Gothic and Renaissance motifs. Three are finest German Renaissance, and of them the most memorable without doubt is the tall, rather effete King Arthur ('an English hero', says the guide,) who, resting on his shield with an easy nonchalance, seems the epitomy of the sang-froid normally associated with the Anglo-Saxon character. His figure, considerably taller and leaner than most of his companions, illustrates how early the stereotype of the Englishman abroad was set. The figure of Maximilian himself, kneeling in prayer, seems less memorable, and one is immediately aware that whoever fashioned Arthur was convinced of this hero's unique qualities – a man apart, who could in no way be mistaken for Theodorich the Ostrogoth or Dietrich of Berne.

In a small corner of the church there is another monument, so self-effacing as to merit little more than a glance. A small marble tablet, neglected save for a few dried up wreathes, records the loss of South Tyrol, the most beautiful part of the Alps which, despite its predominantly German-speaking population, was ceded by the secret Treaty of

London in 1915 to the Italians. Despite Italy's disappointing performance during the Great War, Rome was able to demand the territory at the peace conference of 1919 (after taking the precaution of occupying it first), and South Tyrol has proved a minor problem in the way of good relations between Rome and Vienna ever since. To a certain extent this has been solved by the granting of a fair degree of autonomy to the province, but the visitor to Tyrol should bear in mind that while there are many who are reconciled to Italy ruling 200,000 Tyroleans, they are far from happy about it, and this small tablet is as much a national shrine for them as Maximilian's lavish tomb.

Next to the plaque is another monument to Tyrol's irrepressible spirit of independence and heroism, in the tombs of the province's hero Andreas Hofer and those of his two lieutenants, Speckbacher and Haspinger. In 1809, the year which saw 'Phaeton fall' at the Battle of Aspern, the Tyrol witnessed another spectacular set-back for Napoleon's armies when the population rose up against the French and the Bavarian auxiliaries and routed them at the first battle of Berg Isel. The leader of the uprising was the tall, massive Andreas Hofer, a cattle trader by profession always attired in the traditional costume of his valley. Hofer was the Alpine Austrian's hero *par excellence*. He knew how to exploit the mountains for defence, and how to set off avalanches for attack. Most important of all, he was able to turn a peasantry armed only with billhooks and crucifixes studded with nails into a disciplined fighting force. But, a true Alpine child, he was clumsy in bureaucracy and his instincts were always those of the warrior rather than of the diplomat. He had, as Richard Rickett has observed (in *Austria's History*, 1972), only the haziest notion of Austrian nationhood and his outlook never ranged very much farther than the mountain peaks of his native land.

Three times the men and women of Tyrol rose up with Hofer to drive the invader from their soil, but these victories had a bitter conclusion. Although Hofer had been victorious and had installed himself in Innsbruck as *Oberkommandant*, Napoleon in the wake of his costly victory at Wagram demanded that the Austrian emperor sacrifice the Tyrol. To his eternal shame the emperor conceded. When peace was signed at Schönbrunn on 14 October 1809, Hofer still had faith in the emperor's promise that a peace which separated Tyrol from Austria would never be agreed to. He could not believe the rumours of the peace treaty. 'Tyrol', he wrote to the emperor, 'is ready to shed the last drop of her blood for Your Majesty.'

Once more the Tyrolese rose up, but this time the news of the armistice with Napoleon divided them and their lack of unity enabled them to be scattered and defeated. Hofer was captured, taken to Mantua and shot on Napoleon's instructions the following February. The people who had risen four times in furious revolt against a numerically superior enemy in defence of their land and their Kaiser deserved better treatment from their emperor, and the memory of Vienna's betrayal lingers even after the passage of 170 years. The tombs of Hofer and his lieutenants are a permanent symbol of defiance and of Tyrol's contempt for distant Vienna.

From the suburb of Wilten, with its two spectacular Baroque churches, a train, once red and white, now after baneful modernization little more than a tram, ascends the Stubaital to Krieth and the mountains where every peak beckons southwards to the Dolomites. On the way a stop can be made at Berg Isel, the site of Hofer's resistance. A museum recalls his adventures and the history of that crack fighting unit of the First World War, the '*Kaiser Jaeger*' regiment.

On the other side of Innsbruck there are two places which can be visited in half a day. Hall is a complete town of the same period as the centre of Innsbruck, with parts of the city wall and moat extant. The town owes its prosperity to salt, and a visit to the salt mines is a traditional excursion here. Some of the interminable caverns are rumoured to extend so far underground as to afford the chance of fleeing across the not too distant German frontier.

Not far along the line to Kitzbühel lies Rattenberg, a busy city of wrought iron signs and Gothic alcoves on the banks of the Inn. Innumerable castles seem to crown every surrounding peak, a memorial to the Inn valley's function as a traditional invasion route. Of these Schloss Tratzberg, first mentioned in 1300, is the most impressive, with all its Renaissance and Gothic courtyards. Rattenberg itself merits a good hour's attention; its prosperity alas has resulted in the over-restoration of many buildings, though several streets have survived unchanged by the march of time or tourism.

Moving further west towards Vorarlberg, the character of the Tyrol becomes less distinctive and the Alps have little to distinguish them from those of eastern Switzerland. The inhabitants sound and look Swiss, too, and it is not surprising that the Austrians of this province have on several occasions during their recent history expressed the wish to become part of Switzerland. The province is prosperous and industrialized. The capital, Bregenz, lies on the shores of Lake Constance. Near by, the second most important city, Bludenz, is the headquarters of the Austrian chocolate industry. Only in one small village, thirteen miles from Bregenz, is there a small but precious reminder that the visitor is still in a part of the Austrian Alps. In Hohenems a brief but glorious festival of Schubert lieder steals some of the limelight from Salzburg each summer.

The combination of music and mountains is of course more celebrated in Salzburg where, during the easter and summer seasons, the streets resound to what is arguably the most famous music festival in the world. As well as being the venue for this cultural activity, the city is also, by virtue of its geographical position, the headquarters of many West German industrial concerns in Austria. Indeed in Salzburg the *Anschluss* is still a reality. German currency is accepted in many restaurants and shops and there is considerable German economic investment in the city, helped by the fact that it is in the nature of its inhabitants to look west rather than east.

It is often overlooked that the city which is the most visited in the country has only been a part of Austria since 1816. Before then it was a German archbishopric. Mozart thus was not born an Austrian, though his long periods of residence in Vienna made his music clearly more Austrian than German. At the principal railway station in the city the proximity to Germany is underlined by the presence of West German customs formalities for those travelling west, and by the sudden appearance for those sitting on a through train of vast numbers of West German conductors and ticket collectors, who self-importantly invade the train, taking it over from their shabbier and more easygoing Austrian counterparts.

The Austrian flavour of the city is, however, unmistakable. Though the festival has become a vulgarized affair, even at its height there can be few more quintessentially Austrian sights than the view from Nonnberg at sunset when the cupolas and towers of all the city churches strike up the Angelus. The Baroque architecture of the city, in comparison with Vienna, is refreshingly restrained. Fischer von Erlach's masterpiece in the city, the Kollegien Kirche is a magnificent example of an almost austere Baroque style which can also be admired in his three other churches in Salzburg, and which is often overshadowed by the opulence of his work in Vienna.

Those who arrive at Salzburg and cannot find a room at one of the fashionable hotels should not despair. Down by the river a red marble staircase leads up to what is the only place in the city to offer that combination of old furniture, winding staircases and riverside views that is the hallmark of a nineteenth-century pension. The sixteenth-century Höllbräu guesthouse always seems to have a room available and this comfortable inn has frequently saved at least one English correspondent from spending far too much money on a characterless, overpriced box of a room at one of the nearby luxury hotels.

Höllbräu, though externally recently restored, has remained internally what every guesthouse in Austria once aspired to be before the war. Winding staircases, Biedermeier sofas, mirrors and evocative pictures all give the impression of a down-at-heel, rambling country house. From here the best of the town lies at one's doorstep. The cathedral, the library of St Peter's and the churches of Fischer von Erlach can all be enjoyed after an early breakfast. Beyond the Residenz Platz, named after the palace which today houses a modest collection of paintings, there is the curious architecture of the Festspielhaus. The idea of starting a festival in Salzburg first took effect in 1917 when a *Festspiel* committee was formed under the guidance of Hugo von Hofmannstal, Max Reinhardt and Richard Strauss. In 1920 Nestroy's morality play *Everyman* was first performed in the open in front of the cathedral, and since then this rather overrated work has been a regular feature of the festival.

Above the town loom the vast fortifications of the *Festung* with its rather insane miniature corner chapel looking like the creation of a sinister dream. It is significant that, although few buildings approximate more closely to the popular idea of a castle, its grey mass is never referred to as the *Schloss* or castle but as the *Festung*, the fortifications. A museum here contains several old Austrian uniforms, as well as mementos of the German *Wehrmacht* of the last war. The Salzburg Austrians welcomed Hitler even more enthusiastically than the Viennese. It is no coincidence that the conductor who cuts arguably the most Teutonic figure of any musician alive, Herbert von Karajan, was born in Salzburg. The late Professor Hans Sedlmayr, the learned biographer of Fischer von Erlach and a committed Nazi during the war, taught architectural history here for many years.

The other Austrian city which rose up in delirium for the Nazis was Graz, and to reach Styria from Salzburg we must take the Tauern railway, passing under the backdrop of towering peaks in the crystal air of Bischofshofen before eventually reaching Leoben, celebrated for its Gösser beer. North-east of here lies the junction of the medieval town of Bruck an der Mur, whence half an hour to the south the river Mur accompanies the railway out of the upper Styrian mountains and on to the hills of Graz.

Although Graz was unashamedly nationalist and then enthusiastically Nazi in its history, it remains today the least spoilt of all the Austrian provincial capitals. '*Ville de grâce, aux rives de l'amour*' was Napoleon's laudatory pun in 1809 and it remains apt over 150 years later. The local cuisine, like local manners, outshines that of Vienna, and the narrow streets, unfailingly courteous inhabitants and shuttered windows give the city a lazy southern air. But the Styrian mountains, among them the slightly menacing Schöckel which dominate from the north, reaffirm the Alpine spirit. It is a curious combination, and it gives the city a nineteenth-century provincial air which is very '*K. und K.*' – '*Kaiserlich und Königlich*' (imperial and royal).

In the nineteenth century the city, the second largest in Austria, was known as '*Pensionopolis*', and its streets were filled with pensioners from the imperial bureaucracy and army. When the fruit trees blossom in the spring it still has the healthy atmosphere of a place of retirement. But there is more to the city than this. Graz is not comparable to Edwardian Bournemouth or Carlsbad. Like Innsbruck, it was once a Habsburg capital, presiding from 1564 to 1619 over what was then known as Inner Austria. This comprised the provinces of Styria, Carinthia, Carniola, Gorizia, Istria; significant parts of Yugoslavia and Italy.

From the main Hauptplatz the cobbled Sporgasse leads up to the Franzensplatz, with its ensemble of Biedermeier buildings, and beyond to the Burg. Begun in 1438 by Duke Frederick V, the Burg contains in its first courtyard a unique Gothic double-spiral staircase constructed in 1499. Opposite the unprepossessing main entrance, however, is the Gothic cathedral and the remarkable mausoleum of the Emperor Ferdinand II, built in 1614. It is a romantic building and a significant one for Austria. Its interior decoration was the first work of Fischer von Erlach, and the exterior was the first façade to speak the language of the Baroque in the eastern Alps.

Through a nearby arch is the Stadtpark, an incomparable

collection of trees and walks clustered around the small hill
which stands at the heart of the city and is known as the
Schlossberg. The park was laid out in the early nineteenth
century after the fortifications were blown up in accordance
with Napoleon's wishes after the armistice of 1809. The
French had been unable to subdue the 'wild men beyond the
Semmering', an entire French army being defeated by the
impressive fortifications of the city which were guarded by
only a handful of Austrians under one Major Hacker. But, as
happened in Tyrol, Vienna capitulated and Graz was left to
pay the price. The untaken fortifications were handed over to
the French who promptly razed them. Only the clock tower,
the architectural mascot and symbol of Graz, was spared after
a huge indemnity had been extracted from the populace.

The demolition of the fortifications had one pleasant result,
however – the laying out in the English style of the Stadtpark.
With its bandstand and fountains, chestnuts and oaks, it offers
the most pleasant promenade in summer. In autumn, when
the Styrian festival of contemporary arts takes place, it
resounds to modern plays and concerts. In one direction a
gaslit path leads up to what is in effect a garden in the air. In
another, the Schubertstrasse leads past several eccentric villas
in one of whose gardens a small pavilion rejoices in the
reputation of being the first monument ever erected to
Mozart. This delightful monument has had to suffer the
addition of a tasteless swimming pool from a new owner.

At the end of the Schubertstrasse, the Biedermeier and
mid-nineteenth-century villas peter out through botanical
gardens into a dense wood known as the Leechwald. It is one
of the great joys of the city that within a few minutes of the
centre there is completely unspoilt country.

Through the Leechwald a dozen or so paths penetrate the
forest. They all lead eventually to the pilgrims' church of
Maria Trost, a lovely Baroque building in yellow stucco. *En
route* it may be possible to find, surrounded by trees, the rather
neglected café with its old engraved windows and faded
parquet which for decades has welcomed travellers, the

charming Roseggerhof. The once equally picturesque
nineteenth-century observatory, whose burgundy-coloured
lookout was a familiar landmark peering from the tops of the
woods, has been ruthlessly restored in bright aluminium. But
this is virtually the only eyesore to be seen in or around Graz,
and the streets of Geisdorf and those around the magnificent
neo-Gothic Herz-Jesu church have been virtually untouched
during recent decades.

In the unpretentious but civilized opera house the lavish
interior is the perfect backdrop to performances of operetta
which are generally more professional than those to be seen in
Vienna's Volksoper. Near by, the Theater-Café with its
impassive Magyar pianist continues to evoke a 1920s atmosphere. The heady music, with potent draughts of hot
chocolate mixed with rum, render resistance to seduction
futile. In this twilight world an Austrian newspaper editor can
suffer moods of devastating gloom because in an important
article he forgot to mention and thank a particular civil
servant. In the same way, the omission of his academic title in
print can assume catastrophic dimensions for both sub-editor
and chief editor.

In Graz we rarely leave the world of the tragi-comic. The
head of an influential department in the local bureaucracy
seems a likeable buffoon, and indeed is to all intents and
purposes; but his face displays the scars of his student sabre
days, and in the dark streets around the university the curious
initials and exclamation marks of pan-German student clubs
are daubed on many of the walls.

The pan-German element in Austria's students has always
been strong in Graz and it imparts to the city a Teutonic
flavour lacking in Vienna. The citizen of Graz is aware of its
age-old role as an outpost of Germanic culture, though the
southern climate and the proximity of the Balkans have
worked their magic; in no other city in Europe save the Saxon
settlements of Transylvania is the Teutonic element so gentle
and well-mannered.

In nearby Carinthia the German influence is altogether

more hearty, making the generally inward-looking Carinth-ians somewhat volatile and prone to fanaticism. The country-side of Carinthia, with its lakes and towering Karawanken mountains, no doubt encourages this extremism, though one should not forget that it was also the inspiration for many of Brahms's most sublime melodies.

A few miles south, in the very shadow of the Karawanken peaks, craftsmen continue a century-old tradition of making exquisitely engraved shotguns in the village of Ferlach. To the north, towards Vienna, stands a series of fortresses, including Hochosterwitz, once the great bastion of the duchy of Carinthia. So eccentric and meandering is the layout of the main railway line between the capital, Klagenfurt, and Vienna, that this castle can be glimpsed between the peaks twice over a period of thirty minutes as the train makes a long irrelevant curve around it.

For all its Alpine charm, however, Carinthia will not detain us for long. In order to round off our tour of western Austria we must retrace our steps to Lower Austria and spend a night in a monastery. There are several of these establishments here, and most offer rooms to the traveller if he announces his arrival in advance. At some he may feel compelled to rise with the sun for lauds, but at others neither abbot nor monk will look at him askance if he feels unable to face plainsong at 5 am. At lunch the food and wine will be excellent. He will be met from the nearest bus stop by a nun armed with an umbrella to help him walk if necessary in heavy snowdrifts or rain through icy Baroque courtyards to rooms which will equal a luxury hotel in style and comfort and surpass it in good taste. An entire year could be spent happily week-ending in these splendid institutions which combine the calm of prayer with some of the greatest architecture in central Europe. The frescos at Altenburg, the library at Melk, the food at Heiligenkreuz – all these are at the disposal of the traveller based in Vienna.

Admittedly, monastic life may not be to everyone's taste, so after perusing the abbey of St Florian's near Linz, the dismal polluted capital of Upper Austria, we should withdraw fifteen miles up the river Enns to Steyr, whose inhabitants eke out a living from iron as they have done since the Middle Ages. The main square of this little-known town is a museum of beautiful Baroque and Renaissance houses. In one of the houses Bruckner composed his Sixth Symphony, but otherwise the town has been neglected by itinerant genius. Near by, a narrow-gauge steam railway will take us to Schloss Rosenegg, a humble but prettily situated house behind which lies one of the most charming inns left in Austria. If the atmosphere here is to the visitor's taste, he should drive on to the wine town of Retz near the Czech frontier, and head east till he reaches Fratres with its abandoned railway line still trying to cross the iron curtain into Moravia.

Envoi

Some weeks after completing most of the text for this book, I returned for a couple of days to Graz. Threading my way through the Baroque houses behind the Herrengasse, I encountered by chance an old Austrian I had first met many years ago. He was now very old and not a little fragile. In 1978, glass of schnapps in hand, he had extolled the virtues of the Treaty of Berlin a hundred years earlier. Beneath a large portrait of Disraeli – surely the only one in Austria – he had dwelt on the need to keep the portrait in a prominent position throughout the year, 'as a reminder of the great services to the Austrian empire performed by Disraeli in supporting Austria's occupation of Bosnia-Herzegovina a hundred years ago'.

Fluent in many languages, schooled in the history of central Europe, in his combination of charm, eccentricity and cosmopolitan interests he represented the best of the Austrian spirit. He showed no trace of self-aggrandizement or insincerity, though at the same time he used his words with spectacular wit and style. That such characters have survived in Graz, if not in Vienna, is surprising. More surprising is that they continue to exist side by side with the most hostile and anti-intellectual forces. As I walked back to the inn overlooking the Mur an hour later, an astonishing sight loomed out of the darkness in front of the Schlossberg. On a poison-green flag a nearby projector beamed out a swastika. As it dominated the empty streets, lighting up the sky, the sheer grotesqueness of the image was overpowering. Suddenly the projector changed, and a Turkish crescent replaced the swastika; it was obviously the misguided creation of some member of the Styrian autumn arts festival.

It was a relief to see that the swastika was not the result of neo-Nazi activity, but it was disconcerting to discover that some of the citizens of Graz saw nothing wrong in lighting up the sky with a symbol that epitomized their country's extinction and was much more evil than anything that had been visited on Austria during its long history.

The following day I saw that at least one inhabitant of Graz had done the right thing and had smashed the window through which the projector had shone its sinister image. It was a gesture as winning as Christopher Plummer's ripping up of the swastika flag erected outside the von Trapp family villa in *The Sound of Music*, the film which, for all its obvious frivolity, captured precisely the dilemma of the Austrian patriot whose fellow countrymen saw nothing wrong in 'just getting along', as Max the entrepreneur in the film insists.

Perhaps because the Austrians stare such paradoxes in the face every day they have developed a keen sense of reality in which nothing is as it seems, and herein lies perhaps the great and unique charm of the country. Fantasy and imagination run riot for those who wish to escape the constant restrictions of narrow-mindedness and crassness which confront one at every corner. Thus, while refusing to greet one's neighbour with a '*Grüss Gott*' is tantamount to a tacit declaration of war, no one will prohibit a fifteen-mile toboggan ride down a mountain at three in the morning, or a nocturnal game of cricket using one of Fischer von Erlach's Trajan columns outside the Karlskirche for a wicket. None the less, perhaps because life for most Austrians is an exercise in comfort, an obsession with making little things as difficult as possible also flourishes, *viz.* the disgruntled landlady, the pedantic bureaucrat, etc. And yet where else in Europe is it possible to find that one has become an *habitué* of a coffee house after only a few visits, and be brought the desired coffee before one has even caught the waiter's eye? Where else, on the other hand, does the waiter's calm imperturbability dissolve into hysterical anger when some little thing goes wrong in the kitchen?

Some would point out that such paradoxes are inevitable in a country whose mentality has been fashioned by centuries of exuberant Catholicism. Certainly Catholics, especially those who travel behind the godless Iron Curtain into lands where Catholicism is on the defensive, feel much relief at encountering a land in which worship is both so easy and so welcome. Few people who remain in Vienna on a Sunday can fail to escape being woken up by the sound of bells calling the faithful to mass, whether in the spectacular Baroque of the Piaristenkirche or its unforgettably tranquil side chapel, or in the Mechateristen monastery a few streets away where the age-old dialogue between priest and acolyte is performed for a silent congregation. Here the spirit can find succour, a rare luxury in Vienna, and countless souls have been saved from despair on that greyest of grey days which is a Viennese Sunday in winter.

High up above the city, in a landscape as dramatic as anything John Buchan describes in *John Macnab*, a narrow-gauge railway winds its way up to the pilgrimage town of Mariazell. The *Gemütlichkeit* encountered here quickly dispels the frustrations and furrowed brows of Vienna, and reminds us that for all the vices and vicissitudes on which I have dwelt, Europe would be a poorer place without the Austrians.

Index